1999

A NOVEL

Stanley C. Baldwin

INTERVARSITY PRESS
DOWNERS GROVE, ILLINOIS 60515

InterVarsity Press® is the book-publishing division of InterVarsity Christian Fellowship®, a student movement active on campus at hundreds of universities, colleges and schools of nursing in the United States of America, and a member movement of the International Fellowship of Evangelical Students. For information about local and regional activities, write Public Relations Dept., InterVarsity Christian Fellowship, 6400 Schroeder Rd., P.O. Box 7895, Madison, WI 53707-7895.

All Scripture quotations, unless otherwise indicated, are taken from the HOLY BIBLE, NEW INTERNA-TIONAL VERSION®. NIV®. Copyright ©1973, 1978, 1984 by International Bible Society. Used by permission of Zondervan Publishing House. All rights reserved.

ISBN 0-8308-1363-2

Printed in the United States of America ♾

Library of Congress Cataloging-in-Publication Data

Baldwin, Stanley C.
   1999: a novel/Stanley C. Baldwin.
     p.   cm.
   ISBN 0-8308-1363-2
   1. Radio broadcasters—United States—Fiction.   2. Talk shows—
United States—Fiction.   3. Prophecies—Fiction.   I. Title.
   II. Title: Nineteen ninety-nine.
PS3552.A4517H4   1994
813'.54—dc20   94-16540
                                                     CIP

15   14   13   12   11   10   9   8   7   6   5   4   3   2   1

04   03   02   01   00   99   98   97   96   95   94

Acknowledgments

The kind cooperation and help of the following is hereby gratefully acknowledged:

Sgt. Derrick Foxworth, Det. Marilyn Schulz and Sgt. Larry Neville, Portland Police Bureau; Glenda Langager, Rape Survival, Inc.

Paul Linnman, KATU-TV, Portland; Lew Davies, KPDQ, Portland; Sandy Snavely, KPHP, Portland.

Barbara Martin and Jeannie Taylor, author's intensive critique team.

Krystal Brown, Roberta Hegland, Elsie Larsen, Linda Moxley, Joe Ryan, Maria Tolar, Kay Carpenter, Geneva Iijima, Kathy McAlister, Pam Ravan, Patricia Smith, Cindy Wilkinson, Dan and Elizabeth Hamilton, John Desjarlais, John Bibee, critiquers.

Cynthia Bunch-Hotaling, editor, InterVarsity Press; Al Jannsen, Steven R. Laube, Roger Smith, editorial and marketing advisors.

Note: In this work of fiction, the following real people appear in roles comparable to their real lives: Marilyn Schulz, Paul Linnman, Lew Davies. Other names and characters, as well as the incidents portrayed, are products of the author's imagination and used fictitiously.

1

Matt Douglas wasn't the type to snooze away his mornings, though he had proven through twenty years of marriage that he could shave, shower and dress without being fully awake. This morning, however, he had actually dozed in bed for a few minutes after his alarm had announced it was wake-up time Monday morning. Or perhaps he'd dozed only seconds—dreams don't take long. In any case, while half-asleep he had seen *an angel.*

The angel was a diminutive fellow, all white, just sitting in midair, looking relaxed and pleasant. That's all there was to Matt's dream. The angel did nothing, said nothing.

Matt awakened and stretched, smiling with amusement at the thought of the laid-back little guy.

Matt's wife, Priscilla, was already eating her breakfast of coffee and toast when Matt reached the kitchen. He paused beside her chair to kiss her good morning and run his fingers through her dark shoulder-length hair. Matt proceeded with his usual breakfast routine: start with two-thirds of a cup of water and a dash of salt in a saucepan, cover and boil vigorously, then add one-third cup of rolled oats. As he let the cereal rest two or three minutes—good nutty oatmeal has to *ripen,* as he called it—Matt told Priscilla about his angel dream. "It was weird!" he concluded.

"Sounds like a nice angel to me," Priscilla said with bright eyes and a funny little smile. "What's so weird?"

She knew Matt would have a good answer. He had breezed through Bible college with mostly A's, and he knew his Bible as well as most preachers. Privately, Priscilla thought Matt knew almost everything as well as any man alive.

Matt recognized Priscilla's expression as meaning *here it comes, all I ever wanted to know about the subject and more.* He launched into it anyway. "Every angel you read about in the Bible was on a specific mission. Usually announcing something big. Like when the angel Gabriel told Mary she was to become the mother of Christ. Or like when the angel told Abraham that God was going to destroy Sodom and Gomorrah with fire and brimstone. But this angel didn't say anything." Matt paused. "And he didn't look like he had anything on his mind either."

"Well, you said you only saw him for a moment," Priscilla observed. "He didn't have time to say anything. Anyhow, even an angel would be allowed to rest sometimes, wouldn't he?"

"I suppose." Matt sprinkled two teaspoons of brown sugar on his oatmeal, and poured on nondairy creamer—his one concession to what he considered a diet-food fad. "But he shouldn't be resting at the same time he's appearing to me. Really, 'Scill, not once in the Bible do you see an angel just sitting back, knees crossed, relaxing. Angels are called 'ministering spirits,' and *ministering* means *serving,* not sitting down on the job."

Matt was half-joking and half-serious. "That's it," he said. "I saw an irresponsible angel." Even as he said it he discounted the idea, for how could an angel be irresponsible—actually disobedient to God— and still be an angel? It didn't make any sense.

But why should it make sense? Matt thought. *It was just a dream.* He had other things to think about. "Well," he said, "whether my angel was irresponsible or not, I can't be. Got a 'really big shew' today. My guest on 'Hear and Now' is John Profett." Matt pulled a publicity release from his briefcase and read aloud: "Not since *The Late Great Planet Earth* has a book exploded with such impact. Millions now believe Jesus Christ must come soon. Examine the evidence for yourself. Read *1999* by John Profett."

Priscilla snickered. "John Profett? Give me a break! That's a phony name if I ever heard one. A book on prophecy by a guy named Profett? How obvious can you get?"

Matt nodded indulgently. "Sure," he agreed, "it probably is a pseudonym. So what? Ever hear of Mark Twain?"

"Okay, honey," she said, rising to kiss him. "Maybe you're right." She would soon be on her way to McKinley School, where she was teaching fifth grade for the second year. With their kids, Diane and David, both gone to college, the Douglas family needed the extra income a lot more than they needed Priscilla at home all day. Matt would leave later for his job at Oregon Christian Broadcasting, known as KOCB to listeners.

"See you this evening," she added. "You will come home this evening, won't you? You won't follow this Profett guy out into some desert place to wait for the end of the world?"

Matt chuckled. "Very funny. He's not like that at all. I interviewed him six months ago, before he became so famous. He's very sane and level-headed." Matt paused. "More important, so am I."

"I know you are, dear," Priscilla said. Just before closing the door gently behind her, she added, "And it's a good thing, because I'm not too sure about him."

Matt knew she really did have confidence in his judgment, but he also felt patronized; if there was one thing Matt had proved, it was his discernment. Few people could match his record when it came to spotting phonies and seeing through specious claims. One of the best-received series ever broadcast on "Hear and Now" was his "Before You Buy What They Are Selling." In it he offered tips to help listeners evaluate all kinds of true-sounding claims, ranging from ads for over-the-counter drugs and other consumer products to the pronouncements of politicians and preachers.

He was also proud of his most noted achievement, an exposé of the World Trust Bank. This "bank" had taken in over eighteen million dollars from church members in Oregon and Washington. The bank officers, also active church members, had promoted their enterprise mostly through churches and Christian organizations, including advertising on KOCB.

It sounded so good. Investors were promised interest payments significantly above market rates on their investments, and all net profits from the bank would go to finance world missions. Early investors unfailingly received exactly what they were promised, and the bank flourished.

Matt and Priscilla even considered investing some money themselves, but Matt was uneasy about the whole thing. He began investigating, interviewing the bank's officers and checking into the bank's investments. What he uncovered, after much effort, was a typical "Ponzi" scheme, in which early investors were paid with funds received from later investors. The "bank" had no real assets and most of the money was siphoned off for the personal use of the owners.

For exposing the World Trust Bank Matt received the prestigious Bradbury Award for Investigative Journalism. And the so-called bankers went to jail.

Though Matt was immensely gratified at winning the Bradbury, it seemed to him now that it had never really done him much good. After some four years, no networks or big city stations had come courting him to work for them. No political organization had recruited him to run for high office. No one had even asked him to sit on the governing board of a big corporation or nationally known ministry.

* * *

Matt looked up at the clock on the wall of the KOCB studio. 3:45. Just then Shelly Green, the receptionist, presented her appealing blond-framed face at Matt's office. "Mr. Profett is here," she announced, and vanished again.

Matt walked out and thrust his hand toward the black-bearded, stocky man who rose from a couch to meet him. Though the man stood about five feet nine or ten, two or three inches shorter than Matt, he looked to weigh every bit of Matt's 190 pounds. "Mr. Profett, good to see you again. A lot has happened since you were here last."

"Call me John," the man replied, smiling warmly. "Yes, it's staggering to see how the Lord is using this little book." He extended a copy of *1999* to Matt, who declined it and displayed his own copy.

"Your publisher sent it, and I read it," Matt explained. "The interview today will be much like the previous one, except this time we're giving you the entire hour. I know our listeners want to hear what you have to say."

"Fine," said Profett, "but are you sure you don't want this copy? I've already inscribed it to you personally."

"Well, in that case, yes, I certainly would like it, and I appreciate it," Matt said. "Thank you."

During the interview, Matt focused on the central theme of Profett's book. "Tell us why you believe Christ will return in 1999," he said.

Profett responded with captivating warmth and intensity. "I have many reasons—and very good reasons—for my beliefs. Second Peter 3:8, referring to Christ's return, says, 'With the Lord a day is like a thousand years, and a thousand years are like a day.'

"That verse, Matt, is the key to understanding the prophecies of Christ's return. As you know, God created the heavens and earth in six days. Scripture says a day is like what? Like a thousand years. The six days of creation correspond, then, to 6,000 years. And guess what? Almost exactly 6,000 years have now passed since Adam was created in 4004 B.C.

"Now, then, on the seventh day God rested, and that corresponds to the thousand-year reign of Christ on earth mentioned in Revelation 20:6. That time of rest called the millennium is due, and Christ obviously must return to earth before he begins his reign here."

Matt was ready. "So you take literally Peter's words about one day being like a thousand years to the Lord. But even so, isn't that 4004 B.C. date for Adam based on faulty calculations? *Unger's Bible Dictionary* says so; it dates Adam 'perhaps as early as seven or ten thousand years B.C.,' and I believe the Hebrew chronology also dates him at over 5000 B.C."

"Well, one thing is clear," said Profett, sounding like he'd just won the debate, "those two sources that differ with the 4004 date can't both be right, can they? It's true that Ussher's chronology, the source of the 4004 date, has been discredited by some. But it's important to understand how Ussher arrived at his date for Adam. He calculated it from the biblical genealogies in Genesis 5—11. Now, Unger and others say this Genesis chronology is incomplete and has no validity for dating Adam. They insist that archaeological facts contradict Ussher's chronology."

"Right," said Matt. "So how can you still use the 4004 B.C. date and say that six 'days' or 6,000 years have elapsed since the time of Adam?"

"Because, don't you see, the only thing that matters here is God's word. It doesn't matter whether Genesis 5—11 leaves out some generations—or even centuries. God has his own way of counting time, and his timetable is revealed in Scripture. The fact that man's best calculations differ is completely irrelevant. As the very same passage in 2 Peter points out, '*By God's word* the heavens existed and the earth was formed . . . *By the same word* the present heavens and earth are reserved for fire, being kept for the day of judgment.' The figures given in God's word add up to a 4004 date for Adam, and God's reckoning is everything. Christ will return when God says."

"And that's in 1999?"

"Yes—or as I've said all along, within three and a half years one way or the other. Because, don't forget, the date for Adam was 4004 B.C., not 4000. And Bible scholars agree that Christ was born about 4 B.C., making it just 4000 years from Adam to Christ. Now there's some coincidence! But that would make the sixth day end in 1996. See, as Scripture says, nobody knows the exact day or hour when Christ will come."

"All right," said Matt, glancing at a computer screen which read *Don—Hillsboro,* "let's take some calls. We have Don on the line from Hillsboro. Go ahead, Don, you're on 'Hear and Now.' "

"Hello, Matt, Mr. Profett. You know, I'm really concerned about this book and the near hysteria it's generating. Some people—it's all they want to talk about, and I hate to think what will happen as the year 2000 draws closer. Then, even when 2000 passes, we'll still have people upset for three-and-a-half years more before they will know you were wrong—like all those who have come before you purporting to prove Christ's coming was at hand."

"Be careful, Don," replied Profett. "You sound a lot like the skeptics described in the very same passage I've been quoting. Second Peter 3:3-4 says, 'In the last days scoffers will come. . . . They will say, "Where is this 'coming' he promised? Ever since our fathers died, everything goes on as it has since the beginning of creation."' Scoffing at my message is, in itself, a fulfillment of Peter's prophecy."

"I'm not scoffing," said Don. "I just don't want to see a lot of people get hurt. I—"

"But you see," Profett interrupted, "Christ is coming. And even though others have mistakenly expected him earlier, it will happen at some point. Right? That time is fast approaching, and you don't want to be among those who mock."

"Thank you, Don, for that call," said Matt, working to give his guest the last word. He noticed Profett was unfair in rebuffing Don, but his guests frequently overstated things, especially when responding to critics. That was okay. Strong convictions strongly expressed made for a good talk show.

Later, the interview completed, Matt shook hands with Profett again and thanked him for coming. However, Profett had something more on his mind. "You know, Matt," he said slowly and deliberately, "I don't believe it's coincidence that my book promotional tour began and ended here with you. I've been thinking about something I'd like to talk over with you. Could we have lunch or dinner sometime soon?"

"Sure, I'd like that," Matt said. "When did you have in mind?"

"Well," said Profett, "how about right now?"

Matt raised his eyebrows, thought a second, then nodded. "Why not? Let me wrap up a couple of things and I'll be right with you."

Returning to his office, Matt slipped his new copy of *1999* along with his notes and media packet into the file. He dialed his home phone and when the recorded message ended with a beep, he said, " 'Scill, it's me. I'll be a bit late. I'm going to dinner with John Profett. 'Bye."

At Chen's restaurant, the two men split one order of sweet-and-sour shrimp and one of cashew chicken. Matt raised the subject of the Portland Trail Blazers and their prospects for winning the NBA championship, but Profett said he wasn't a basketball fan. Matt mentioned the North American Free Trade Agreement and how he thought it might benefit the Pacific Northwest. Profett listened politely but obviously had little interest.

Then Profett came abruptly to the point. "Matt, what would you think about coming to work with me?"

"Well, I don't know," said Matt, keeping his excitement hidden. "In what capacity? I have to tell you, I like my job at the station. I am doing what I enjoy, and it's a real ministry, too."

"This *1999* thing has really exploded on me." Profett was talking on as if he hadn't heard a word Matt said. "I can't handle all the requests for appearances on radio and TV, and that's just the Christian stations. Now more and more opportunities are opening on commercial radio and TV, too. I have a tremendous open door from the Lord, Matt, and I need a man like you, a committed Christian who knows his way around the media to direct and manage me."

"I'm flattered," said Matt, "but you don't know anything about me. I—"

"Matthew Crawford Douglas," Profett interrupted. "Born May 27, 1952, in Portland, Oregon. Raised in a Christian home by your maternal grandparents, Ben and Bess Crawford, after your father and mother were killed in an auto accident when you were three. Graduate of Multnomah School of the Bible in Portland, 1972. Received your B.A. in journalism from the University of Oregon in Eugene, 1975. Married fellow student Priscilla Marie Brown of Portland in June 1974. Father of two children: Diane, a student at George Fox College, and David, a student at Multnomah. Talk-show host and the only journalist in Christian media ever to win the Bradbury Award for Investigative Journalism." He paused. "Shall I go on?"

Matt stared. "Well, I am impressed. You not only dug up all that information but also memorized it?" Matt didn't mention that he felt more than a little uneasy at being the object of such scrutiny.

"It's important to me, Matt. You are important to me. I also know that you have a real heart for the things of God." Profett paused. "I wonder if you have any idea what a staggering opportunity this is. Christ is coming, Matt. He's actually coming! And right now I am the one he's using to announce it. I know that sounds fantastic, but it simply is a fact. The whole country is being turned on its ear by my book."

Matt sat shaking his head in disbelief. He knew *1999* was making waves nationally, but he could hardly imagine Profett wanting him as personal manager. Still, he had won that Bradbury . . .

Profett was talking on. "Look, Matt, I have no delusions about myself. I am a common ordinary man. But so was John the Baptist. God chooses ordinary people so he will get the glory. If I were to drop the ball and fail God now, he would raise up someone else. In fact, I expect he will raise up someone else anyhow to confirm the message, but I'll explain that later. Right now, I'm his choice. And you are my choice, Matt. Tell me you'll consider it and pray about it. That's all I ask."

"Well, I guess I can pray about it, but—"

"Tell you what; I'm taking the next month out to pray and prepare myself for what's coming. One month from today, Matt—one month—I'm going to need you on board. Meanwhile, let's meet in a week or so to see how things are developing."

Matt nodded agreement, and Profett said, "Let's commit all this to the Lord in prayer." Without waiting for a reply, he bowed his head. "Almighty God, thou art Lord of all and we are thy servants. Thank you for allowing us to live and to serve you in these critical last days. In a world that has turned its back on you, we pray that we may always be found faithful. In the name of Christ we pray. Amen."

After they had parted, Matt hesitated about going straight home. He needed to think about it, and wasn't ready to talk to Priscilla. He drove around for about an hour, and reached home about ten. As he expected, Priscilla was already in bed asleep. "Hey," she said drowsily as he climbed into bed, "what's the big idea? We agreed you weren't going to follow this Profett fellow off into the desert to await the end of the world."

"Chen's isn't exactly the desert," said Matt. "We had dinner and we talked." He leaned over and kissed her cheek. "Now, go back to sleep."

In moments Priscilla was sleeping again, but an hour later Matt was still staring at the darkened ceiling, his pulse racing. *Christ will come again. Why couldn't it be soon? Why couldn't God choose John Profett and Matt Douglas as messengers? All my life I've wanted to do something really great for God. Could this be it? I think I've been faithful in the little things—is God about to set me over much? Maybe the Bradbury is finally paying off. This decision won't wait long. A month. Sooner than that. I have to give two weeks' notice to quit.*

Suddenly Matt remembered his dream of that morning. "Hey, little angel," he murmured, "if you have a message for me, you really need to deliver it." For the first time in hours, he relaxed and smiled. "I am going to be talking to your boss a lot these next few days, and this bit about you just sitting silent and relaxed is likely to come up. I really would hate to see you get in trouble, okay?"

With that thought Matt drifted off to sleep.

2

A week's worth of concern boiling in her mind, Priscilla Douglas looked impatiently at the classroom clock. If she left school promptly at 3:25, she could carve out two hours for herself and still be home when Matt got there. She took her purse from the drawer, arranged the top of her desk, and waited for the bell. When it sounded, the students cleared out quickly, and as soon as the last fifth-grader disappeared from view, Priscilla slid through the classroom door.

The teachers' lounge was just down the hall between Priscilla's room and the main entry. She dashed in to freshen up. *Time for a cut and a perm,* she thought as she pulled a brush quickly through her loosely curled hair. She applied a fresh coat of Very Berry lipstick and dabbed some Liz Claiborne perfume behind each ear.

She adjusted the waistband of her dark pants, tucked in her white blouse, pulled on her red wool blazer, and turned sideways to view her still-girlish figure in the mirror. *Regular exercise and careful eating do pay off,* she thought with satisfaction. Priscilla had found the payoff especially sweet when she and Diane wore each other's clothes. The two were sometimes taken for sisters, a fact that amused Diane and immensely delighted Priscilla. And occasionally one of Priscilla's students would say in awed tones, "You're beautiful, Mrs. Douglas."

The late October afternoon greeted her only moments after the day's final bell. Priscilla headed her white Honda Accord out of the school parking lot toward the upscale suburb known as Hidden Springs. Within fifteen minutes she pulled into the driveway of a newer, well-kept, mountain-view home. Marshall Brown opened his front door as Priscilla reached the steps, and she hurried inside into his embrace.

"We have to talk," Priscilla said. "I've been about to go crazy these past few days." She continued in mock anger, "What's the big idea being out of town when I needed you?"

"Forgive me," Marshall said with weighty tones. "If only I had known, I never would have gone. President Clinton could have waited." Then he turned serious, taking her arm and ushering her in. "What is it, sweetheart? What's wrong?"

Priscilla's father was still a giant to her, even now at age sixty-four. His once-red hair had mostly turned gray, but apart from that, and ever-bushier eyebrows, he had made few concessions to the years. Priscilla appreciated his physical strength, his emotional stability, his control of himself and his circumstances. To Priscilla as a child, he had seemed to rule the whole universe and had eased her trouble with only his presence.

She knew his human frailty now, and had long since learned to cope with her own problems. But sometimes it sure helped to have Dad around. These last two years since her mother's death, she had cherished the relationship with her father all the more, realizing she wouldn't have him around forever.

"You know who John Profett is?" Priscilla asked as she sat down in an easy chair facing her father on the couch. "He's the author of that controversial new prophecy book, *1999*." Seeing her father nod in recognition, Priscilla went on. "I'm wondering what you think of him."

"Not a whole lot," said her father. "Why?"

Not ready to answer the *why* quite yet, Priscilla continued to probe. "So, you don't believe he's right about Christ coming back in 1999? Or you just don't like him?"

"I think all this date-setting is ill-advised," said Marshall.

Priscilla was both reassured and pleased to hear that her Dad's thinking paralleled her own, but she wanted more ammunition so she played devil's advocate. "Well, you know, Profett doesn't set a date," she said. "In fact, he's quite careful to emphasize that no one knows the day or hour of Christ's return."

"Bah—that's just a smoke screen!" said Marshall.

Priscilla smiled at her dad's vehement response. "Why a smoke screen?"

"Because it's a flagrant example of following the letter and not the spirit of God's Word. Of course, Profett's not so stupid as to directly contradict what Jesus said about no man knowing the day or hour. But the whole thrust of what Jesus said, repeatedly, is that we will not know when his return is imminent."

Priscilla's countenance darkened and she frowned. "The trouble is, Profett is hardly alone in claiming to see signs of the times. I hear messages like that from reputable preachers all the time."

"True, and in my opinion, most are misguided."

"Well, what do you say to the claim that people are converted by these messages about Christ's imminent return? I know people myself who give that testimony. And according to Matt, many people have come to Christ through reading *1999*. They've told Profett so."

"That's a tough one," Marshall acknowledged. "But we can't decide what to believe and teach simply on the basis of what seems to 'work' in converting people. We are supposed to stand for the *truth.*" He shook his head, leaned back on the couch, and began to expand on his theme, as Priscilla had hoped he would. "You know, sweetheart, every few years for as long as I can remember, someone has come along with a convincing argument about current events being a sure sign that the end was at hand.

"Way back in World War II, when I was only a teenager, we had this radio preacher down in Eugene. I mean, he was *convincing.* Mussolini was the Antichrist, who had revived the old Roman Empire, and Christ's return was at hand. How could anybody doubt it?

"Well, of course, after the death of Mussolini and the defeat of the fascists, the guy was pretty much discredited. He dropped out of sight for a while, but then he came back bigger than ever, preaching a new version of his cocksure—and I might add cockeyed—prophecies.

"People are converted through 'end-of-the-world' preaching, you say, and maybe some truly are. But I wonder how many are turned away from faith by these endless cries of wolf. I know your Uncle Charley became a lifelong skeptic after the Eugene preacher I told you about sold him on that Mussolini stuff."

"Well," said Priscilla, "you haven't exactly relieved my mind." She glanced out the living room window at Mount Hood looming white against a graying autumn sky. Then, deciding to tell him everything, she faced her father again. "You see, Profett was on Matt's radio show last week, and he invited Matt to go to work for him—some sort of personal manager and media consultant role—and I'm afraid he just might do it."

"Hmmm," her father murmured, frowning and raising one bushy eyebrow in a characteristic expression of concern. "Matt's always been pretty sensible. I can hardly believe he'd do anything rash."

"That's what *he* keeps telling me," Priscilla said, "but for him to even seriously consider joining Profett scares me." She paused. "It's not just that the guy's into prophecy; I don't know why exactly, but I don't trust him."

"And you think Matt's serious about joining him?"

"Well, he spends every minute he's home either poring over *1999*, or praying, or telling me how much sense the book makes and how much he's impressed by Profett. I mean, he hasn't watched TV, he hasn't read the newspaper, he hasn't even—well, let's put it this way, he comes to bed late and gets up early and only kisses me when he's going or coming through the front door. So you tell me if he's serious."

"Sounds like we have a problem," said Marshall. "Have you told Matt how you feel about all this?"

"I've tried, but you know Matt. He's a typical male." She paused. "No offense, Dad; you're not like that. Not as much, anyhow," she added mischievously. "But Matt always says feelings aren't enough; he wants hard evidence."

"Well, then, that gives us a place to start, doesn't it? Let's check out Profett's reputation and character. He could be a con man for all we know. Let me make a few phone calls and see what I can learn."

"Good!" said Priscilla. "Can you do it right away? Matt's supposed to meet with Profett again day after tomorrow, and even if he doesn't give a definite answer then, he will have to make his decision soon."

"Hey, I'll call right now."

Priscilla followed her father into the kitchen and sat at the table as he picked up the phone and dialed. After a moment he said, "Hello, Cindy, how are you today? This is Marshall Brown. Is Pastor Carl in? I need to speak with him."

While he waited, Marshall explained to Priscilla, "My pastor knows a lot of people throughout the Christian community. If anybody can get us the straight stuff on Profett, he can."

"Great!" said Priscilla. "I've already checked with our pastor, and he doesn't—"

Marshall interrupted silently, holding up his hand and engaging in conversation with someone she assumed to be Pastor Carl. She waited expectantly until her father hung up the phone. "Well, he doesn't know anything either," Marshall told her, "but like I said, he can find out. He will get back to me in a day or two."

Priscilla didn't mask her unhappiness about that prospect. "Meanwhile, I guess, I'll just have to wait and pray—some more."

"Well, no," said her dad thoughtfully. "We have other options. We can make other inquiries. Given the seriousness and urgency of the situation . . ." He left the statement unfinished, reached for the phone book, and looked up the Portland Police Bureau. He dialed the number and asked for Captain Rodney Drake.

"Oh, Dad, this is hardly necessary," said Priscilla.

"No, no, it's no problem," said her father. "Captain Drake is a friend of mine."

"Rod, how are you?" he said warmly moments later. "This is Marshall Brown." The men exchanged small talk briefly, and then Marshall explained his purpose. "How would you suggest we check out the background of a person we suspect might not be all he seems?"

They talked a bit more, then Marshall covered the mouthpiece and turned to Priscilla. "He's connecting me with a Detective Connor of the Fraud Detail. Says he's the best one to help us."

Hearing only one end of the conversation that followed, Priscilla again waited impatiently. *The detective must be saying something of significance,* she thought hopefully, *as long as it's taking them.* At last she heard her father express his appreciation "for all the help." He said something about being back in touch soon, hung up the phone and turned to Priscilla. His eyes told her there had been no breakthrough. John Profett was obviously not a known con artist. Of course, she had never imagined that he was. Clearly, they weren't going to find their answers this easily—she had known that—but time was so short.

"Detective Connor has no information about Profett, but he is willing to help us. To do that, he needs some things from us."

"What kind of things?"

"Fingerprints might help. Profett's full name and date of birth. The FBI operates something called the National Crime Information Center. Connor said he could run the name and date of birth through their computers, and if Profett has a criminal record, we'll soon know it.

"However, if the name is a phony, nothing will show on the record, of course, and that's why he wants prints, so he can check the man's identity through the FBI."

He paused, and Priscilla could sense he was being tentative, that he had something discouraging to tell her.

"What else did he say, Dad? You don't seem very optimistic about our learning anything."

"He said not to get our hopes too high, because a lot of people don't even have fingerprint records. If the man was ever in the military or the Peace Corps, if he's ever been bonded or had a security clearance, or been a lawyer or operated a nursing home, they'll have his prints. Otherwise—"

"Operated a *nursing home?"* Priscilla interrupted.

"That's what he said."

"I thought that these days Big Brother knew everything about everybody," Priscilla said.

"He says that's fiction. If a person wants to conceal his past, and especially if he's been lying for a long time, it can be very difficult to positively identify him, let alone know all about him."

"Sounds like there's not much use even trying this approach," said Priscilla.

"Well, there could be lots of use. We might learn a great deal about him. At least we'll know if he's got a record. But can you get his fingerprints?"

Priscilla stared at her father for a moment, then replied, "Sure, I'll just lure him to some nightspot for drinks and I'll swipe his glass and bring it here and you can rush it down to Detective Cooper or Copper, or whatever his name is." She paused, as her father looked at her dubiously. "No! I can't get his fingerprints," she said in frustration. "I've never even met the man."

Marshall was not a person easily deterred from a task. There had to be some way to get John Profett's fingerprints, and he intended to do it. "But Matt has met him," he said, "and plans to see him again—when did you say—day after tomorrow? Hmmm. All right, here's what I want you to do."

3

Matt, I went over to see Dad yesterday." Priscilla and Matt were just finishing dinner, and she knew this was the time to talk to Matt—at the table, before he disappeared for the evening into his study, as he had every night since this Profett thing began.

"And?" said Matt, reaching for a toothpick.

"And I told him I was worried about you going to work for John Profett."

"And what did he say?"

"He said he couldn't believe you'd do anything rash."

"Well, that was nice of him. I guess I still rate a vote of confidence from one member of the family."

"He also said he'd help check out John Profett for us," said Priscilla, ignoring Matt's slam.

"I think I'm quite capable of doing that myself," said Matt. "Let's see now, who won the Bradbury, me or your dad?"

"I don't see how it can hurt to have a little help," said Priscilla, "especially since the time is so short. Are you looking into his background, his character, his reputation? So far I get the idea you've concentrated on checking out his message, but what do you really know about the man? I mean, it can't hurt to gather all the information we possibly can. He certainly checked you out; you said he knew all about us."

Priscilla was pleading her case with intensity, but it wasn't necessary. Involving Priscilla and her dad wasn't a choice Matt would have made on his own, but if they wanted to do some digging, he wouldn't object.

"I'm all for checking him out, honey," Matt said. "You're right that the more we know, the better. If there are any unpleasant surprises, I need to uncover them before I team up with him, not after."

"Oh, Matt, I'm so glad to hear you say that! Because—well, Dad has already done a little investigating, but," she grimaced, "he has an idea and we really do need your help."

"First, I think you'd better tell me about the 'little investigating' your dad's already done," said Matt.

"We haven't learned much," said Priscilla, electing to leave out any reference to the police just yet. "Seems Mr. Profett is something of a mystery man. He's single, as far as anyone can tell. Lives alone southeast of here near Colton, about as remote as he could get and still be only thirty miles from downtown Portland.

"Dad's pastor checked with the little community church Profett attends there." She dug out a small spiral notebook in which she had jotted the pertinent facts. "The pastor says Profett showed up three years ago. He attended regularly until he got his book published, and since then he's been on the road most of the time. The only unusual thing the pastor could think of was that Profett seems brilliant and knows his Bible, particularly the Old Testament, exceptionally well. The pastor thinks Profett may be Jewish, but he's not sure."

"Nothing very sinister in all of that, huh?" said Matt. "So now what does your dad want us to do?"

Matt listened as Priscilla explained her father's plan. Matt was to arrive a few minutes early for his dinner engagement with John Profett the next evening. He would offer the maitre d' a few bucks to see that Profett's drinking glass ended up in a brown paper bag instead of in the dishwasher. He would also learn Profett's date of birth and any other personal information he could.

At this point, Priscilla had no choice but to tell Matt what she planned to do with the glass. "The police!" he exclaimed. "For Pete's sake, Priscilla, why drag them into this?"

"It was Dad's idea," said Priscilla. "I told him it was unnecessary. But he's got this friend on the force, and he called him, and one thing led to another. They want Profett's date of birth and they want his fingerprints."

Matt sighed. "Well, if he has nothing to hide—and I hardly think he's a criminal!—I guess he shouldn't mind us doing a little probing."

*   *   *

Saturday evening Priscilla waited impatiently for Matt to come home from his dinner engagement. He entered, and waved a brown paper bag at Priscilla. The big smile on his face said, "I did it!"

"Wonderful!" said Priscilla excitedly. "Hey, if you want to change jobs, maybe you should become a detective."

The smile faded. "I don't think so," said Matt. "I'd be lousy at questioning suspects."

"It didn't go well?"

"I learned practically nothing," said Matt. "Not even his date of birth. I thought I was being subtle too. I said if I was going to represent him properly to the media, I would need to understand his background, where he was coming from. I said a good place to start was with a biographical sketch."

"That seems reasonable. He didn't go for it?"

"He saw through me instantly," said Matt. "In fact, in our conversation from that point on, I'm afraid he got more information out of me than I got out of him."

"What information? He already had our complete family history."

"Well, he asked me how you felt about his job offer. I had to tell him you weren't too happy about it. Then he wanted to know if you were investigating him, or if that was my idea. Apparently he somehow discovered someone has been making inquiries about him out there at Colton. It was embarrassing."

"So what did you tell him?"

"I told him it was your father's doing, and that I hoped he'd understand that your dad was just trying to watch out for his little girl.

Then I asked him if he didn't think I had a right to know more about the man I might be working with closely in the near future."

"Good," said Priscilla. "You got off the defensive and put the focus back on him. And what did he say to that?"

"He said, yes, he understood why I was asking about his background. He said he was born in Palestine of Jewish parents back before Israel became a state in 1948, so there are no records of his birth. I started to ask about his immigration to America, but he cut me off. He said that I have a right to know those things, and if I decide to join him, he'll answer all my questions. Then I'll understand why he couldn't tell me earlier."

"Well, I must say, that sounds a little fishy," Priscilla mused. "Don't you think so?"

"It doesn't sound good," Matt agreed. "But Profett said we'll understand once we know the facts. So, at this point, since we simply don't know what the facts are, we can't come to any firm conclusions. But we do have his fingerprints. Let's see what we find out from them."

✳   ✳   ✳

Monday morning Priscilla's father stopped by McKinley School to pick up a brown bag containing a water glass. His plan was to drop it off at police headquarters on the way to his downtown office, where he worked as senior vice-president of JBC Investments. He was the "B" in JBC, along with the other founders, Jenkins and Caldwell.

"By noon we should have Detective Connor's report," he told Priscilla. "Drake says the police have a new system that can identify a person from fingerprints in a fraction of the time it used to take. It's called AFIS— Automated Fingerprint Information System. I guess it's really good."

He paused. "Why don't you give me a call during your lunch break?" With that her father said goodbye and left, carrying the brown paper bag. Priscilla thought how incongruous he looked—like a dignified executive carrying his lunch schoolboy fashion in a paper sack.

As she turned her attention toward her class, Priscilla breathed a prayer of thanks for her job. These fifth-graders would give her plenty to occupy her thoughts until noon. Otherwise, she'd probably go crazy waiting.

At noon Priscilla hurried to a phone and dialed her father's number. When she heard his voice on the other end of the line, she said, "Hello, is this the Marshall Brown Detective Agency? This is your rich and beautiful number-one client calling. Do you have any news for me?"

"Well, yes, I have a fingerprint report, Ma'am."

"Good," said Priscilla, "so do we know now what a certain young man named Matt should do?"

"What he should do is find another place to eat besides the Prime Cut."

"What?" said Priscilla. "I'm talking about the fingerprints."

"I'm talking about the fingerprints, too," said her father. "They belong to a man named Robert Allen Pressler. Born in Columbus, Ohio, in 1967. A high-school dropout who's been arrested for shoplifting, auto theft, selling marijuana, assault, and robbery. He did two years in the Ohio State Pen on the assault charge. Seems he beat up an old woman in the street when she wouldn't let loose of her purse."

"Oh, for Pete's sake," said Priscilla. "They obviously gave you the wrong man's record. Born in '67? That would make him less than thirty years old. Profett has to be over forty. Did you tell Detective Casper that?"

"I told him. He said there was no mistake on the report; the only fingerprints on that glass not so smudged as to be worthless just don't belong to Profett. They belong to Robert Allen Pressler, busboy at the Prime Cut."

As she hung up the receiver moments later, Priscilla didn't know whether to laugh or cry. Their detective work had been a farce, but her concerns were as serious as ever—and now time was running out. Matt had to make his decision.

She had to make her decision as well. Was she going to continue fighting this thing? It would be devastating to oppose Matt if he ultimately decided working with Profett was something God was calling him to do. For her to just give in and go along with him would not be much better. A man needed his wife to back him one hundred percent. But how could she support a choice she still felt deep inside was a terrible mistake?

4

As they cruised along the freeway in her boyfriend's vintage Olds 442, Diane Douglas indulged in an admiring look at the young man behind the wheel. Larry Forrester was such an appealing blend of capable man and vulnerable little boy! The dark wavy hair, the intense manner, the sincere and easy laugh, the self-doubt which others might never guess but she had learned to recognize—all of these things were a part of that mix.

She definitely enjoyed the view. They had been going together ever since meeting at "Jesus Northwest," a big summer festival held each year near Vancouver, Washington. While not engaged, Larry and Diane did have an understanding. They would both finish college, and then see if they still carried such strong feelings for each other.

Today they were traveling north on I-5 from Portland to Olympia, Washington—Larry's hometown. The gorgeous fall day lived up to its billing as Diane's favorite season. Here and there the vine maple flashed a brilliant red among the various yellows and oranges of the other deciduous trees. And always in the background was the deep dark green of the magnificent towering Douglas firs predominant in the area.

Larry had mentioned once, back when they first started seeing each other, the fact that her last name was the same as those patriarchs of the great northwest forests. "Are they named after you?" he had asked.

"Of course not," she had said before adding slyly, "They were named after my father."

They had both laughed then, and Diane had never bothered to learn the true source for the name of the tree. She was pretty sure, though, it had nothing to do with her family.

Larry glanced at her and started talking—again—about the fantastic book he had been reading. "Diane," he said, "you've got to read this book. It's called *1999,* and it shows that Christ is coming soon."

Diane really hadn't had time for it, though she wanted to read it. By the time she squeezed her textbooks hard enough to get the kind of grades she wanted—"not necessarily *all* A's"—she didn't have time for much other reading. After all, spending time with friends and family and Larry was important too. She would read that book when she got a little time. Maybe between terms.

Besides, Diane could sense that Larry was talking about anything that came to mind—no doubt to cover his nervousness about her meeting his parents for the first time.

"Relax, Larry, why are you so uptight? Are you afraid your folks won't like me?" she asked with a mischievous grin.

"Hardly," said Larry. "But there's a very good chance you won't like them. I guess I'm afraid you might think the apple doesn't fall far from the tree—that with parents like them, I couldn't be much of a Christian."

"I am insulted," said Diane. "Do you really think I would judge you by your parents, Larry? I admire the way you have stood for Christ alone in your family."

The two could hardly have been from more different backgrounds. Larry's parents were still together, but that was about the best that could be said for them. Larry's father was a domineering man who drank and ran around, but kept his timid wife on a very short leash.

Larry had been converted to Christ through an active youth group at a local church in Olympia. He was at Portland State on a football scholarship, and was considered certain to go high in the NFL draft. Although Larry hoped to play professional football, he was planning to attend seminary too, with pastoral ministry in mind.

But part of his attention was focused on George Fox College, a highly regarded Quaker school in Newberg, only thirty-five miles west of Portland. It was just the right place for Diane, getting her out on her own away from her folks, yet keeping her close enough for frequent visits.

"I don't know where I'd be today if I hadn't been raised in a Christian family," said Diane. "I think you've done just great."

Larry smiled. "Thanks," he said, "but I can't picture you as anything but a strong Christian despite your family. Your dad told me once that you were every parent's dream from the time you were born. You hardly gave them a moment's concern."

"Well, of course he might be just a little bit prejudiced," said Diane. "Short memory, too." She laughed. "I remember one night in my teens when my folks were plenty concerned."

"I don't believe it!" exclaimed Larry. "What did you do, leave the cap off the toothpaste?"

"Well, yes, I probably did, but my folks were more upset about me sneaking out at night to meet my boyfriend, Mark."

"Oooooh, I don't know if I want to hear this or not! Come on, tell the truth; you're making it up, aren't you?"

"Would I lie?" asked Diane, wide-eyed in feigned shock. "Of course I'm not making it up. I went out my bedroom window about eight, met Mark down the block, and we rode around until ten. Unfortunately, my mother caught me trying to sneak back in."

"Really?" said Larry. "Wow. What happened? My dad would beat the tar out of my sister if she ever pulled a stunt like that."

"Dad was pretty upset at first. He asked me in his very strictest voice what in the world I was thinking. I told him that obviously I *wasn't* thinking or I wouldn't have done anything so stupid."

"And that was it? He didn't ground you or forbid you to see this Mark again or threaten to beat him up?"

"No, I guess he figured a first offense only called for a warning." She paused, then added with mock seriousness. "Of course, I've been watching my step ever since then because he might not treat a second offense so lightly. You'd better watch yourself, too, Mr. Forrester."

"Oh, I will, I will!" said Larry. "And now prepare yourself to meet my parents; we're only three blocks from home."

A few minutes later Diane found herself saying hello to a tired, faded woman whom Larry introduced as his mother, Jean Forrester. To Diane's surprise she found herself immediately liking this woman, who seemed so genuinely happy to meet her. Diane had thought it would be hard to respect a woman who would allow herself to be so mistreated, but only now did Diane realize how much she had failed in her effort not to judge.

"Where's Dad?" Larry asked.

"I—he—I'm sure he'll be here, Larry. He knew you were coming." She glanced at the clock. "Excuse me, I'll be right back," she said, and she hurried from the room toward the back of the house.

"Checking on dinner," explained Larry softly. "It has to be ready promptly at six. Then she has to keep it ready until Dad gets home, whenever he feels like coming."

About fifteen minutes past the hour, Larry's father came in the back door. "You should be impressed, Diane," Larry said as his mother hurried to meet her husband. "He's seldom home this promptly."

Moments later Diane saw a paunchy middle-aged man with thinning dishwater-colored hair come into the living room. Mr. Forrester tossed his jacket to his wife, who dutifully hung it in the hall closet. "So, Larry, how's the preacher boy?" he said. His gaze fell on Diane. "And this beautiful woman must be Diane. Why haven't you brought her home sooner?" He shook Diane's hand and held it until she pulled away.

The rest of the evening followed the same pattern with Mr. Forrester alternately belittling Larry, making demands on his wife, and clumsily trying to charm Diane. With every beer he became more obnoxious. About eight o'clock Larry excused himself and Diane, pleading the long drive back to Portland.

"See why I was worried?" Larry said when they were well on their way.

"Yes," Diane said quietly. "But Larry, you are not your father." She paused, then gave him a poke in the ribs. "And you'd better not ever act like him, either."

*   *   *

"What is it with this Profett guy?" Priscilla demanded, after telling Matt about the fingerprint fiasco. "We are getting nowhere. Is he really slippery or are we just that inept?"

"Maybe it's a little of both," said Matt. "I did a little more investigating today—even called his publisher—and I got nothing. Every inquiry I make seems to net the same result—a big fat zero. I guess no news is good news, though. We haven't learned anything negative about him."

He shook his head. "It's strange, 'Scill; it's almost as if the guy dropped in from out of nowhere."

Priscilla furrowed her brow. "Well," she said, "there has to be a way. Maybe we should confront him. Demand his fingerprints." Her voice softened and became uncertain. "Or maybe you can get him to handle some money or documents."

"We could go that route," Matt said slowly, and then he added, "again," for emphasis, "but it looks to me like the only way I'm going to learn much about John Profett is from him."

"But he said he would only tell you about himself if you joined him," protested Priscilla.

"That's right," said Matt.

"No!" cried Priscilla. "Matt, you can't!"

He rose to stand behind her, and began rubbing her shoulders. "Honey, we have no reason to distrust the man, and his book makes a lot of sense to me. By the way, I talked with Diane about it, and she's excited for me. She says most of the students at George Fox—especially the more spiritual ones—think Profett's book is great."

"You told Diane your decision before telling me?" said Priscilla. "When was this? Where was I? I suppose David knows more about it than I do, too."

"Diane called this morning," said Matt, holding up his hand. "Right after you left for school. She wanted to tell us about her visit to meet

Larry's folks. You did leave a little early this morning, you know. Anyhow, I didn't exactly tell her my decision; I told her about the offer, and that I was seriously considering it. She said I'd be crazy to pass up such an opportunity."

"And you're going to take the advice of your daughter?"

"Diane is a wise and insightful person for her age," said Matt. "You've said so yourself. Anyhow, I'm not relying on just her advice. Look, I went along with you on all the detective stuff, didn't I, and where has that gotten us?"

Priscilla had no answer, and Matt didn't want to hear it anyhow.

"I've prayed about it, 'Scill," he continued more quietly, "and I think this is what the Lord wants me to do."

Priscilla looked at him helplessly. What could she say that would outweigh divine guidance?

Matt saw the disappointment in her face. Clearly she didn't understand what was going on inside him. "Honey," he said, "throughout the Bible, when God called people, they offered some reason they couldn't respond. I don't want to do that. What would I say? 'My wife doesn't like the idea'?"

Sensing that Priscilla was weakening, Matt plunged on.

"Please, 'Scill, this could be my chance to get out of a dead-end job into something really big."

"Dead-end job?" echoed Priscilla. "I've never heard you complain about your job before. You like your job. At least, you did."

"I like the work," said Matt, with a little more heat in his words, "but not the prospects. I'm never going to get beyond 'Hear and Now.' That's pretty obvious. My so-called recognition there hasn't meant diddly. I haven't complained before, because I'm not a complainer."

Priscilla just shook her head, obviously unconvinced.

"Okay, suppose I *am* wrong about Profett," Matt persisted. "Suppose I go to work for him, and then learn something unsavory about him. Or suppose I just change my mind, for whatever reason. I can quit, can't I? I mean, it's a job, for Pete's sake; I'm not going to marry the guy."

Priscilla looked at him searchingly. "Aren't you, Matt? You've been so wrapped up in this thing already that I feel like you're more married to him than to me."

"Oh, don't be ridiculous!" said Matt, "If I've neglected you lately, it's just while I've been under pressure to make this decision. Even the Bible says a husband and wife should 'not deprive each other except by mutual consent and for a time, so that you may devote yourselves to prayer.' "

"I know it says that," Priscilla replied. "I also notice something there about 'mutual consent.' I don't remember consenting to anything—or even being asked."

"Okay," said Matt coolly. "I thought it was understood between us without being stated. If not, I'm sorry."

It was clear to Priscilla that Matt still thought she had understood, and that he wasn't really sorry. Deep down inside she had to admit she had understood, but she resented his presumption. And now he was making a major decision she didn't agree with.

What was she to do? Everything about this Profett business seemed wrong to her, including her own reaction to it. If only the whole issue could go away, and things be like they were before John Profett came along. But it appeared that things were going to get worse, not better. Matt was going to say yes to Profett.

5

Matt told Profett his decision the next evening over dessert and coffee at Denny's Restaurant. "That's great news," said Profett. "It's an answer to prayer. I believe the Lord is going to use you greatly, Matt. Far more than you even imagine."

"I hope so," said Matt, taking the last bite of his cherry pie. "Frankly, I'm not real clear about what you expect of me."

"The main thing I want—and it's a need I feel very keenly—is for you to help me plan and carry out the best strategy for getting my message out. To do that, you need to know all about me and about the call of God on my life."

Matt inwardly breathed a sigh of relief. Apparently Profett was about to follow through on his promise to reveal his mysterious background. Matt had feared he might have to wheedle it out of him bit by bit. He had no stomach for that, no patience to play games.

"What I am about to tell you," Profett continued, "is in strictest confidence. You will reveal this information to no one, not even your wife, except as we jointly decide to make it known. Is that clear?"

"You're the boss," said Matt. "It's your information. What you tell me in confidence will go no further."

Matt waited for Profett to continue, but the man sat silent for so long that Matt began to feel uncomfortable. He didn't know whether Profett was weighing his words, changing his mind, or having a spell of some kind.

At last Profett spoke, hesitantly, unlike Matt had ever heard him talk before. "I—I don't quite know, or . . . you see, Matt, you are the only person in the world I've—" He stopped and stayed silent again for a long moment. "Let me start all over," he said at last. "How convincing do you find the message of *1999?*"

"It's quite convincing, but not absolutely convincing," said Matt. "I know you expect me to be honest with you and not just to say what I think you'd like to hear."

"Certainly!" said Profett. "I'm counting on you to be honest. But go on, tell me—what do you find less than convincing?"

"Well," said Matt, "your entire case is based on your interpretation of the Scriptures. While your interpretation is plausible, and very well argued, it is not the only plausible interpretation of the passages and is therefore not absolutely convincing."

"Exactly!" said Profett with an enthusiasm that seemed out of place for a man just told of the weakness inherent in his message. "Exactly," he repeated. "You see, Matt, I have not yet presented my strongest evidence, not in *1999,* and not in my speaking."

"Why not? What is this 'strongest' evidence?"

"*I* am," said Profett.

Matt squinted at Profett. "*You* are?" he finally said. "As far as I know, the Antichrist is the only person who could prove Christ's coming—and that's only by showing up on the scene."

At Matt's mention of the Antichrist a strange look flitted across Profett's face and was gone before Matt could read it. "You are wrong about that," Profett said. "You know, it's incredible how selective most Christians are in their use of prophecy. They all latch on to the same few prophecies—about wars and earthquakes, about the rebuilding of the Temple, the revival of the Roman Empire and the rise of the Antichrist—and they ignore, or they are completely blind to, other prophecies.

"I guess that shouldn't surprise me," Profett continued. "It was the same way at Christ's first coming. The Scribes and Pharisees, who should have recognized his coming, missed it completely."

"So what are you saying? What prophecies are Bible teachers ignoring? And how does your appearance on the scene prove anything?"

John Profett opened his Bible to the last page of the Old Testament. "I think you'd better read this for yourself," he said, handing the open Bible to Matt and pointing to the last paragraph of Malachi.

"See, I will send you the prophet Elijah before that great and dreadful day of the LORD comes. He will turn the hearts of the fathers to the children, and the hearts of the children to the fathers; or else I will come and strike the land with a curse."

Matt looked up from the book into Profett's face. His mind was only beginning to frame a question about the message he had read, when Profett said, "Today this Scripture is fulfilled before your eyes."

Matt went silent and blank for a long moment. "You—you are Elijah?" he managed to croak finally.

"I am," said Profett. "I know this may be hard for you to grasp. So you see my problem—whether, or how, I should reveal my identity to the world."

Matt just sat stunned. "You—*you* are *Elijah*?" he said again.

"Yes," said Profett simply. "I understand that this comes as a bit of a shock to—"

"You are Elijah?" Matt said again. "Elijah? You?" Then he gasped as Profett slapped him in the face with his napkin.

"Snap out of it, man," said Profett. "Look, you need a little time to digest what I've told you. I'm sure you're going to have all kinds of questions once you get over this initial shock. Why don't you take a day or two, go away alone and get your bearings. Then we'll talk again."

Matt nodded in silent agreement, and for several long moments both men just sat there.

"You'll be okay now, won't you?" said Profett as he finally prepared to leave.

Matt nodded again and rose to his feet.

"Remember," said Profett, "what I've told you is strictly confidential."

"Don't worry," said Matt. "I won't tell a soul."

Who would believe me if I did? he thought. *They'd lock me in a rubber room.*

6

att sat in his car thinking for a few minutes. He didn't
know which direction to drive, but he knew where he
couldn't go—home. Priscilla was there waiting for
him, and there was no way he could face her. Not yet.
Not until he had at least begun to process what had transpired between
him and John Profett this night.

Matt started his car and slowly backed out of his parking space.
Instead of heading west toward his Beaverton home he drove east, out
the Banfield Expressway, past Rocky Butte, where he and Priscilla
had sometimes parked overlooking the city when they were dating,
and on into the Columbia Gorge.

Soon brightly lit suburbs gave way to the shadowed cliffs of the
gorge. To the right, far above him in the darkness, Matt could see the
lights of Crown Point, where the old road—once the only route, but
now designated the scenic highway—began its winding, precipitous
plunge down into the gorge. To his left, Rooster Rock soon flashed by,
and a few minutes later, Matt found himself driving into the parking
area at Multnomah Falls. Priscilla and he—and later Diane and David
too—had climbed the steep trail to the top of these high falls at least
once a year. They'd have done so oftener except for the many other
scenic trails they also liked to hike.

Now Matt stayed in the car and watched as floodlights played on
the perpetual motion of the cascading water. He was just beginning to

recover from the shock, but soon he would have to deal with Profett's claim.

"Go away alone for a day or two." That's what Profett had advised, and Matt had silently nodded agreement. Now he saw the absurdity of that idea.

What does he think, that I can traipse off for a couple of days whenever I want? Am I supposed to just leave Priscilla to wonder what happened to me? Or call her on the phone and say, "I can't tell you anything, but I'll be away for a couple of days"? Either way, she'd go crazy.

There was also the little matter of his job at KOCB. He hadn't even given notice yet that he intended to quit. Was he supposed to just show up absent one day?

The most charitable explanation Matt could think of was that John Profett was nearly as upset as he was and unable to think straight. Either that, or the guy had no idea what life was like for a man with a job and family. *Maybe he is Elijah,* Matt thought wryly.

One thing was sure, Matt had to go home tonight. Priscilla was waiting. He couldn't tell her much—he'd given his word—and that was going to make things difficult. But at least he'd be there, as usual. Everything normal, for a little while longer.

Now Matt's mind began to work quickly as he realized with a jolt that he could continue his normal work, too. He had first thought he couldn't possibly do justice to his work and deal with the John Profett issue at the same time. Now it occurred to him that he could schedule guests who would be of most help in sorting out what was happening in his life.

Matt grew excited as he thought of the possibilities. He wouldn't have to betray Profett's confidence at all. No one identified him with Profett yet. And no one knew Profett claimed to be Elijah. He could explore this whole Elijah thing with the best authorities he could find without mentioning Profett.

Matt mentally compiled a short list of possible guests, knowing he could draw from the major seminaries and Christian colleges in the area. First, he would try to get Dr. Jim Zander, the professor of Old Testament at Pacific Northwest Seminary. Zander was very articulate, and as good an authority on the Old Testament as one could find anywhere. Then there was Dr. Elaine Newman at Seminary of the West. Her field was biblical languages, and she would be an excellent guest.

"Hey," Matt said aloud as another great idea hit him, "I could even delay my departure from KOCB for a couple of weeks or a month." The "Hear and Now" program would make a perfect vehicle not only for his personal evaluation of Profett's claim, but also for doing the job Profett wanted him to do.

How had Profett put it? "To advise him on whether and how to make his identity public" or something like that. How better could Matt test the openness of the Christian leadership to the whole concept? He was bound to gain valuable insights on how best to pursue Profett's agenda.

In fact, these two jobs could not dovetail any better. When God was in something, details sometimes came together in remarkable ways. This scenario was beginning to fit that pattern, which suggested that maybe—just maybe—Profett actually was Elijah. After all, Malachi did say Elijah would come again before Christ. If that were true—and certainly the Bible was true—maybe Profett was Elijah as he claimed, and God had specially prepared and situated Matt for his role of working with him. How exciting that would be!

But if he discovered Profett was a phony, that would be dynamite too. He'd be duty-bound to expose the guy—and that would be an even bigger scoop than his series on the World Trust Bank. Maybe then people would sit up and take notice. Maybe then they would realize that a man doesn't win the Bradbury for just anything.

This was beginning to look like a win-win situation. Whatever the truth proved to be about Profett, Matt could come out smelling like a rose.

Right now, however, his most pressing problem was what to do about Priscilla. She wasn't going to like it one bit if he refused to tell her what was going on. Furthermore, unlike the general public, she already knew he was involved with Profett. If he went ahead with his plans for "Hear and Now," she was sure to put two and two together. She might not come up with four—since the truth was so bizarre—but she would come up with something tremendously unsettling to her, and to their marriage.

Well, for tonight I have no choice, Matt thought as he turned his car toward home. *I can't tell her.*

Somewhere along the way another great idea hit Matt. It was so obvious he wondered why he hadn't thought of it sooner. He needed to see John Profett again right away, tomorrow. He could put off Priscilla that long, and if his idea panned out—if John Profett went along with it—he could tell her everything by tomorrow night.

Matt sighed, feeling much better. This had been quite a night, but he was coping actually quite well, thank you.

Matt noticed how different the freeway ahead looked now. On his way out he had been hurtling into blackness, heading away from the city lights. Now driving ever closer to the great metropolitan area with all its illumination was almost like emerging from a cave. The contrast paralleled his inner state going out and in, and he reveled in the growing lightness.

Then he remembered John Profett's words, "Today this Scripture is fulfilled before your eyes," and he was nearly overwhelmed again.

"Elijah?" he wondered aloud. "Elijah?"

7

hanks for agreeing to meet with me again today," Matt said, "and for coming to my office."

"No problem," said Profett. "I was surprised, though, to learn you were working today. You bounce back quickly. I like that."

"I've got some great ideas," said Matt. "At least, I think so, and I want to know what you think. First, I want to bring some prominent Christian leaders on 'Hear and Now' to discuss the prophecy that Elijah is to return before Christ. This will give me an excellent opportunity to gauge how much acceptance there is of the idea, and to get people started thinking about the possibility. Of course, I'll do this totally apart from any mention of you at this point."

"Sounds fine," said Profett. He looked Matt squarely in the eye. "It will also provide an opportunity for you to decide whether or not I'm a phony."

Matt looked away for a moment, but then met Profett's gaze. "Okay, I admit it," he said. "I *am* finding your claim a bit incredible."

"Of course," said Profett.

"On the other hand, if you really are—if you are . . ."

"Elijah," said Profett. "How are you going to help me prove it if you can't even bring yourself to say it?"

"I figure I'll either get more and more doubtful or more and more convinced," said Matt. "Once I'm sure of what I believe, I won't have any trouble saying it."

"Fair enough," said Profett.

"I've got another idea," said Matt. "I understand that you have to be able to trust me with your confidences. It puts me in a real bind, though, when I can't even tell Priscilla what's going on."

Profett was shaking his head grimly. "We can't make exceptions, Matt. A secret told to one other person is no longer a secret." His eyes flashed, and he added, "Especially if you tell a woman!"

"What?" said Matt, not believing his ears.

"Women!" said Profett. "You think I don't know women just because I'm not married?" Seeing the dismay on Matt's face, Profett changed his tone completely. "Forgive me," he said. "You don't understand. I was talking about Jezebel."

"Jezebel?" said Matt, looking doubtful and confused.

"Yes, I was talking about Jezebel. She betrayed our whole nation, Matt, and she betrayed God."

"That may very well be," said Matt, "but I'm not talking about Jezebel; I'm talking about Priscilla. I trust Priscilla, and I'm sure she would keep your secret, but I agree there's always the possibility it could leak out.

"Anyway, it dawned on me last night that some rumors circulating that you are Elijah, or could be Elijah, or claim to be Elijah, might not be so bad. That's what politicians do, you know, when they want to spread some message but don't want to announce it officially. They leak it."

Profett was still shaking his head but less decisively. His eyes were registering doubt, and Matt felt he was making progress in getting his point across. "That would be one way of putting our strategy into God's hands," he urged. "We don't really know how or when to release your message. If I tell Priscilla and she leaks it and the rumor spreads, it could be God's way of preparing people for the announcement."

Matt paused. "And it would sure make things a lot easier on me."

Profett was thoughtful for a few moments. "You are a resourceful man," he said finally. "I think God has shown his hand in directing you to join me. You certainly bring insights to our team that I wouldn't come up with on my own." He took a deep breath. "Okay," he said, exhaling. "There's no point having you with me if I'm not going to listen to you. But tell no one except Priscilla, and make sure she knows it's confidential."

Profett rose and extended his hand. "I feel good about our relationship," he said, as he shook Matt's hand. "We'll make a good team."

Matt nodded, mumbled agreement, and looked awkwardly down at his hand, then fleetingly at Profett's face.

"What is it?" said Profett. "What's wrong?"

"Well," said Matt, frowning, "I never shook hands before with a man who claims to be almost 3,000 years old. The idea takes some getting used to."

Profett sat back down. "Let's talk a little more," he said. "Ask me anything you want. My first priority is to make you comfortable with our relationship."

"Where do I start?" asked Matt. "I've been reviewing everything the Bible says about Elijah. First he was taken up into heaven by a chariot of fire. What was that, a spaceship? Where have you been and what have you been doing for the last thirty centuries?" Now the questions came faster. "How did you arrive here in the United States and why in Oregon? How is it you speak such good English? Can you also speak Hebrew? Can you work miracles? If so, why not just call for a drought on the land or bring down fire from heaven as Elijah did? That would prove your identity, and you wouldn't need help from anyone like me."

"Whoa!" said Profett. "Let's take one question at a time.

"First, you need to understand that I cannot work miracles. I never could and don't imagine I ever will. True, I told King Ahab it would not rain until I said so, and it didn't, for three and a half years. But James had it right when he wrote centuries later, 'Elijah was a man just like us. He prayed earnestly that it would not rain, and it did not rain.' That's James 5:17."

Matt probed further. "But what about the contest on Mount Carmel when you called down fire from heaven and exposed Baal and his prophets as frauds? And—and—the other miracles. I can't think of what they were right now, but I'm sure there were many. Weren't there?"

"No, Matt, there were not many, and when a seeming miracle did occur, it was not by some snap of my fingers, some incantation or some special power. It was a result of earnest and concentrated prayer. I'm a man just like you; I've never claimed otherwise."

"Just like me? I don't claim to be 3,000 years old. What about all that business of your going to heaven in a chariot of fire?"

"Actually, it's closer to 2,900 years old," said Profett. "But as to the chariot of fire, and where I've been, and how I arrived here, I'm afraid you've got me. I can't tell you much. Not that I'm unwilling, but I don't know what happened either. To me, it was a matter of being swept up in an exhilarating ride, and the next think I know it's a whole new scene—modern-day America.

"I guess God must have had me in suspended animation somewhere. Anyhow, I spent the first several months here in America studying the Bible and world history to discover what has happened the last 2,900 years."

"This is crazy," said Matt. "It's just crazy."

"I know," said Profett, sounding discouraged. "See what I'm up against?"

The two men sat silent for a few moments, each lost in his own thoughts. Profett spoke first, his voice subdued. "You know, you said earlier that if I worked a miracle like calling down fire from heaven, that would establish my identity and I wouldn't need you. But you see, Matt, I've been that route and it didn't work.

"Sure," he continued, "it was a tremendous experience to see God answer my prayer, to see that altar go up in flames after we had drenched it with twelve barrels of water."

He paused and his eyes gleamed for a brief moment but then clouded again. "But it didn't change anything. The nation still didn't turn to God. I was never more discouraged in my life than when I realized that the victory at Mount Carmel was pretty much for nothing. I wanted to die, Matt. I *prayed* to die." He smiled. "That was one prayer God never has answered to this day.

"This time around I don't want to make the same mistakes, Matt. I don't know how I can convince this nation, and the world, that God is true and I am his prophet. But I do know that a great demonstration of God's power won't do it.

"That's why I need you, Matt. And this rumor idea of yours is an example of just the kind of thing I'd never think of. It's intriguing!"

Matt rose from his desk. Time was passing, his mind was racing, and he still needed to make final preparations for his afternoon show. "Once again, I really appreciate your coming in," said Matt. "And thanks for being so open with me."

8

Priscilla flipped when Matt told her Profett's big secret—that he was Elijah, whose return had been foretold in the book of Malachi.

She looked at Matt as if he had lost his mind. "I can't believe that you, of all people, would fall for a nut case like that!" she exclaimed.

"Why is he a nut case?" Matt demanded. "You are pretty quick to pass judgment on a man you haven't even met and know nothing about."

"Give me a break!" said Priscilla. "The idea is ridiculous! I'm surprised he doesn't claim to be Jesus Christ, but I suppose that will be next."

"Perhaps you're not aware," said Matt coldly, "that the Bible predicts Elijah will return before Christ comes again."

"So what?" said Priscilla. "Every nut that comes along can dredge up some Scripture to support his claims, no matter how bizarre they are. You know that. Really, Matt, you can't be serious about this."

"I am serious," said Matt, "and all I'm asking you to do is be reasonable."

"Be reasonable?" Priscilla echoed. "I wish you could hear yourself. Here's a man who thinks he has just seen Elijah and he's telling *me* to be reasonable!"

Matt found no more room to discuss it with her. To her, Profett's claim to be Elijah was preposterous, and that was that.

The air cooled quickly between them after that. Matt didn't know what to do, but he hoped that given a little time, she would at least consider the possibility that Profett's claim could be true. Why was it, he mused, that Bible believers had so much trouble accepting what was really quite a clear statement in the Bible?

Meanwhile, he went ahead with his plans, scheduling both Dr. Jim Zander from Pacific Northwest Seminary and Dr. Elaine Newman from Seminary of the West. They would appear on successive programs on Monday and Tuesday of next week, and Matt was looking forward to that with keen anticipation.

He told Priscilla who his "Hear and Now" guests would be and why. That way she would at least see he wasn't heading way out in left field. It had been hard to gauge what effect, if any, his strategy had on Priscilla: she did not respond.

At work on Friday, Matt mulled over the coming weekend and decided it was time to reach out again to Priscilla. Maybe dinner out tonight would help. Otherwise, this was going to be one long, miserable weekend.

When noon came, Matt called McKinley School to invite Priscilla to the Rhinelander that evening. The Rhinelander was one of their favorite dinner spots, with its quaint German decor, wonderful food, and singing waiters and waitresses.

Mrs. Dugan, the office secretary, told Matt that Priscilla wasn't available, but she would give her a message. Matt wondered about that—noon was the one time she usually was free—but he told Mrs. Dugan to have her call him, and then went back to work.

The Friday guest on "Hear and Now" was Cicily Boyd, author of a new book on the Christian attitude toward the environment as opposed to nature worship. Ordinarily, Matt would have been excited about this topic and guest, but now it seemed he was filling time until Monday, when he could get into the Elijah question.

Nevertheless, Matt gave his complete professional attention to the program and didn't realize until it was over that Priscilla hadn't called.

I guess she's more angry than I realized, he thought. *Or maybe she just didn't get my message.* Matt decided to go home early, before Priscilla could start fixing dinner, so they could still go to the Rhinelander.

When he drove into his driveway, Matt was surprised that Priscilla's white Accord was not there. Could she have been delayed for some reason at school? Or had she stopped somewhere on the way home? Maybe she was inside but had left the car at Jensen Brothers for servicing.

Matt went into the house, but found no one there. An hour passed, and then almost two, and still there was no sign of Priscilla. Where could she be?

Matt called the school. A custodian answered and said he thought all the teachers had gone but he'd check. He called back a few minutes later. "No," he said, "I checked everywhere and there are no teachers here. Her car's not in the parking lot, either. I hope nothing is wrong."

"No, no," said Matt. "I'm sure there's a simple explanation, but thanks for checking it out."

Matt waited a few more minutes as the hands of the clock moved toward seven. He hated to call anybody else and get them upset over nothing. On the other hand, this was not like Priscilla at all.

Matt walked to the front door, opened it, and looked through the glass storm door up and down the darkened street. It had been windy all day, and the late autumn leaves had swirled around him in the street as he had driven home. Now, however, a heavy rain had set in, and the rain-sodden leaves were sticking everywhere despite the fact that the wind was still blowing as hard as before.

Matt turned back inside. He went to the telephone and began dialing, then hung up before he had finished. There was no use upsetting Priscilla's father unnecessarily.

Taking a sheet of paper from the notepad beside the phone, Matt wrote, " 'Scill, I've gone to look for you along the route between here and McKinley. Be back soon. It's now 7:12."

He switched the phone answering machine to record an outgoing message. "I'll be back shortly; please leave a message, especially if this is 'Scill calling."

Matt didn't see how Priscilla could have had car trouble between school and home. Businesses and residences lined the way, and she would have called him—unless she'd had an accident.

As Matt drove, he studied the roadside as closely as he could through the wind-blown rain. He watched for the Accord and also for any sign of a recent accident, such as shattered glass in the roadway or on the shoulder. A few minutes later he arrived at McKinley School. *Might as well check the parking lot, too,* he thought, *just to be absolutely sure.*

When his search proved fruitless, he sat with the motor running, trying to imagine where else he might look. Had Priscilla taken some other route home? Had she perhaps gone shopping? Or stopped off somewhere on an errand?

Maybe she had gone to see her father. Matt could drive out there, check for her car en route, and then see if it was parked at Brown's. That way, he could check that possibility without alarming Marshall.

As he drove toward Hidden Springs, Matt racked his brain for some idea of what had happened to Priscilla. Nothing he could think of made any sense. She was angry with him, yes, but not enough to take off somewhere without saying a word. Could she have been a victim of foul play? Until now, he had refused to consider that possibility.

Matt pulled up in front of the Brown residence and looked in the driveway and on both sides of the street. There was no white Accord. The light was on inside the house, and Matt debated briefly before going in.

"Matt!" said Marshall, when he answered the doorbell. "This is quite a night to be out." He stepped out on the porch and looked toward Matt's car. "Is Priscilla with you?"

"No," said Matt, "Priscilla's not with me. I—uh, I thought she might be here. She hasn't come home yet from school."

Marshall looked at his watch. "She hasn't? Why it's after eight. Where do you suppose she could be?"

"Probably home by now," said Matt. "Let's call and see."

Marshall picked up the phone and dialed Matt's number. A few moments later he hung up. "No," he said, "all I got was your machine."

The two men looked at each other, mounting concern showing on both their faces.

"You don't suppose—" Marshall began, then stopped.

"What?" said Matt. "What are you thinking"

"You don't suppose she went out to Colton to see John Profett?"

Matt stared. "The thought never occurred to me," he said. "Why would she?"

"Well, I don't know," said Marshall, "but something was going on with him that she wouldn't even tell me. She said she couldn't because it was strictly confidential, but that it was definitely weird. I've never seen her more upset."

"I'm sure she wouldn't have gone out there," said Matt, "but just on the outside chance, I'll call and ask."

He picked up the phone and dialed. "Hello, John," he said moments later. "I'm glad you're home. You—uh, haven't seen my wife—Priscilla—out there this evening, have you?"

He paused. "That's what I figured," he said, "but I wanted to make sure." He paused again. "No, no, I'm sure she's all right. Probably found a big Friday night sale and forgot to tell me about it. Thanks. Yes, I'll let you know just as soon as we hear from her."

Matt hung up the phone and turned to Marshall. "He hasn't seen anything of her, though I suppose it's possible she drove out there and got lost, or had car trouble. Or even got stuck in the snow; Profett says it's been snowing heavily there for a couple of hours. Boy," he said, frowning, "now I don't know what to do."

"I think you'd better go home so you can be there in case she comes or calls," said Marshall. "Meanwhile, I'll check with the police and hospitals about any accidents that have been reported."

"Okay," said Matt. "I'll call you when I get home. She will probably be there getting ready for bed and wondering what's taking me so long."

All the way home, Matt watched for Priscilla's car. As he approached their street, he half expected to find it in the driveway, and was again disappointed.

When he let himself in the front door, it was obvious that things were just as he had left them. He walked through the house, checking especially their bedroom and the guest bedroom. Priscilla was not there.

Matt went directly to the phone and called Marshall. "She's still not here," he reported. "Have you learned anything?"

"No, I've drawn a blank," said Marshall. "You know, I'm really beginning to get worried."

"So am I," said Matt. "I think it's time we called the police."

"The trouble is, said Marshall, "the police won't usually accept a missing person report until someone's been gone for twenty-four hours. That's why I've already called my friend on the force, Captain Drake. He can get things moving a little quicker. In fact, he's already asked the Clackamas County Sheriff to check the roads up toward Colton for Priscilla's car.

"If she doesn't show up by morning, Drake wants to meet with us, and he also said he might go have a little talk with Mr. Profett."

"Why?" said Matt. "Didn't you tell him I already called and he hasn't seen her?"

"Yes, I told him. But in an investigation, they question everybody, and Captain Drake seems to think Profett's as good a place as any to start."

Matt hung up the phone and sank back into his chair. It was ridiculous to suspect Profett just because the man was a bit different and mysterious. But where was Priscilla? Where?

9

Priscilla received Matt's message from the school secretary, Betty Dugan, that she was to call him, and debated whether to do it. She hated it when Matt acted as he had lately. Earlier in their marriage, she had sometimes brooded for days because Matt was insensitive to her feelings. In recent years, she thought she had grown beyond that. Obviously, she hadn't—not completely. Not if the provocation was bad enough. And this Profett thing was the worst.

She would get over it, of course. She would have to. When Matt thought he was right, he was the most stubborn, obstinate man on earth. "He'll never change!" Priscilla murmured aloud as she furiously erased the morning's lesson from her classroom chalkboard.

Still, she couldn't bring herself to give in to Matt quite yet. So she was supposed to call him, but why should she? Whatever he wanted, it could wait.

Despite her defiant inner monologue, Priscilla found herself going to the office. She picked up the phone and began dialing Matt's work number, but then hung up. Maybe this stalemate would end with her caving in as usual—but Matt wouldn't have it so easy. As far as she was concerned, Matt could wonder for a while. She wouldn't call, and maybe she wouldn't go straight home from school today either. Several stores down at the Lloyd Center were having a big sale—she had seen it in the paper.

When school dismissed, Priscilla headed out of the parking lot still undecided what to do. At McLoughlin Boulevard, she had to keep going straight toward home or turn right toward Lloyd Center. She turned right. So did the car behind her, in which rode three disreputable looking men.

The sales at Lloyd Center weren't all that great. Priscilla wandered through two or three stores, buying only a sweatshirt in one and a frilly blouse in another. She knew she paid too much for the blouse, but she didn't care. Not now. Later, she would probably return it.

She noticed that the mall cinema was showing a film she had been wanting to see. Just last week she had asked Matt to take her, but he was too busy spending every moment on John Profett. *Of course, he's neglecting me only "temporarily,"* she thought bitterly. *Yeah, temporarily for seventeen days now. Okay, so I'll take myself to the movie.*

Priscilla enjoyed the film, and she knew Matt would have liked it even more than she did since it had more adventure than romance. She wondered what he was doing right now. He was probably worried. After all, she was hours late and hadn't even called home. Irritated with herself for feeling guilty over the anxiety she was causing "poor Matt," she thought, *Hmmpph! I hope he* is *worried.*

Once out of the mall, Priscilla turned her Accord toward home. The rush hour traffic had passed and, although snow mixed with the rain that blew heavily against the windshield, she expected an easy drive home.

Two blocks from the theater, Priscilla stopped at a traffic light. Despite the storm and the darkness, city lights dimly illuminated the entire area. She noticed two young men hopping out on the passenger side of the car behind her—apparently they were being dropped off there. Then she saw one dark figure cross behind her car, and before she could even reach for the lock he jerked open her door and shoved a gun in her face. Then the other man opened the passenger door.

Priscilla stared open mouthed, first at one man and then at the other. "Get over," the one on her side ordered as he shoved her and slid in behind the wheel. The other man jumped in on the passenger side, sandwiching Priscilla between the bucket seats.

Priscilla's mind flashed to a particularly horrible abduction she had heard about not three weeks earlier. A woman waiting at a bus stop had been bludgeoned with a tire iron, forced into a car, taken somewhere and raped, then shoved into the trunk of the rapist's car. She had managed to force open the trunk lid and had rolled out while the car was traveling almost fifty miles an hour. She narrowly missed being run over by the car following.

The horror Priscilla had felt when she read the details of that woman's experience flooded over her. Now it was happening to her! She struggled to think rationally. Maybe these men just wanted her car. "Please—let me out," she begged. "You can take the car."

"Did you hear that?" the driver said to his accomplice. "She says we can take the car. Here I thought we already took it!" Both men laughed.

I've got to do something, Priscilla thought desperately. She grabbed for the ignition key with her left hand and turned it. The car lurched as the engine died, but Priscilla couldn't withdraw the key from the ignition.

The man in the passenger seat—a tall gangly fellow with big crooked front teeth—threw both arms around Priscilla and pinned her arms tightly to her side. She could smell his rotten boozy breath as he mouthed a string of curses in her ear.

"Let go of me!" Priscilla demanded, struggling.

"Shut up!" he said. "We're giving the orders here."

Meanwhile, the driver had restarted the car, and in a few minutes they were pulling up in front of a run-down old house in a shabby neighborhood. The man with crooked teeth got out first, cautiously, and then reached in and pulled Priscilla out by the arm. He twisted her arm into a hammerlock and hustled her up the walk toward the front steps of the house. She glanced back, and saw a third shadowy figure talking with the driver. The third man then got into her car and drove it away, while the driver came and followed them into the house.

The sound of her car faded into the distance, and Priscilla's hope faded with it. She was alone in a strange place in the hands of criminals.

"Oh, God," she prayed, "help me!"

10

Sleep was out of the question for Matt as long as Priscilla was missing. Since he had done everything he knew to do, he could now only wait. He turned on the TV and tried to watch, but nothing held his attention. He wondered where Priscilla was at this moment, and fought the mental image of her in trouble somewhere out in this storm. He kept praying she was all right, and he tried to plan what he would do when morning came.

He would have to notify Diane and David, for one thing, but not right away. *But I will call the pastor—he'll get people praying.*

Sometime after midnight, Matt decided he might as well try to get some work done in his office. Monday and Tuesday would be important interviews on "Hear and Now," and he needed to formulate just the right questions to ask his guests about Elijah.

Toward morning he finally dozed off for a while in his recliner in the living room. Before daylight he awoke with a start to realize he had seen his angel again. Matt rubbed his forehead and moved the recliner to the upright position, pondering the meaning of the recurring angel vision.

As before, the angel said nothing and did nothing, but there all similarity to Matt's previous dream ended. Instead of being relaxed, this angel was clearly distressed. Rather than an all-white vision of peace, this angel's entire aspect was dark, not in a sinister vein but dark-soiled, as if he'd fought his way through the legions of hell.

Matt realized at once that his two dreams paralleled the emotional states of the dreamer. A few days ago his life had been placid, like the angel he had seen then. Now he was in turmoil. Probably that was all there was to it; his dreams were reflecting his emotions.

And yet God *had* used angels to warn people. An angel had warned Joseph to take the baby Jesus and flee in the middle of the night to Egypt, when King Herod was planning to kill the child. And there were others as well. If this dream was indeed a warning from God, what did it mean? Priscilla was already missing. As a warning, this dream was certainly late in coming. Another case of irresponsible behavior by his angel? Before, he had found that idea amusing. Now he didn't find it funny at all.

The phone rang just before six-thirty. Adrenaline pumping, Matt leaped to his feet and grabbed the receiver. His heart hoped it was Priscilla putting an end to this ordeal, but his better judgment told him it was not.

"Have you heard from Priscilla?" Marshall asked directly.

"Not a word," said Matt. "Have you?"

"No," said Marshall, "and I can't imagine where she could be. I'll tell you one thing, though. If Profett is mixed up in this, he's going to rue the day he got our family involved in his schemes."

Matt had never heard such anger in Marshall's voice. When he spoke again, however, he was his usual calm, controlled self. "The main reason I called is to tell you that Captain Drake and I are coming over at nine. It's his day off, but he's acting unofficially. He wants to ask us a few questions and get a jump on the investigation if Priscilla doesn't show up today."

"Fine! I'll be here," said Matt.

He hung up the receiver, and the phone rang again under his fingers. "Has your wife come home yet?" Profett asked.

"No," said Matt, "I haven't heard a thing from her."

"I've been praying," said Profett. "All night. She's all right, Matt. The Lord has given me that assurance.

"There's been a lot of snow," Profett continued, "both in the coast range and in the Cascades. She probably got snowed in somewhere and couldn't get through to you by phone."

"I certainly hope you're right," said Matt, "but I don't know why she would have gone out of the city in the first place."

"Perhaps to get away by herself, to think," suggested Profett. "I've sensed there are some difficulties between the two of you—over your new job," he said, stating things obliquely.

Matt did not reply.

"Right?" asked Profett.

"Well, yes, we've had a few problems," Matt admitted.

"But things are going to be all right," said Profett. "And I am going to stand with you until they are."

"I really appreciate that," said Matt, "and I promise to let you know just as soon as I learn anything."

"You don't understand," said Profett. "I am going to stand *with* you. I'm coming as soon as I can get some chains on my car and get in there."

Matt felt immensely grateful. *And to think that I doubted this man.* "Well, that's kind of you, but it's not really necessary—" he began.

Profett would not hear any objections. "Yes," he said, "it is necessary, and I'm coming."

"Well, okay," said Matt. "Just so you'll know, I'm meeting at nine with a police officer who is a friend of Priscilla's father."

"Fine," said Profett. "I should arrive by the time they're done."

After hanging up, Matt pulled aside a drape and looked out into the gray morning. It was still rainy and blustery. He turned on the radio to a news and weather station. "Rain, heavy at times but tapering off toward evening," the forecast said. "Snow accumulations to sixteen inches in higher elevations, and windy with poor visibility." Then the announcer added, "Better stay out of the gorge and the mountain passes, folks, and the way I hear it, even the west hills. But, hey, it's a great Saturday to stay in and do some of those jobs around the house."

*   *   *

At nine on the nose, an unfamiliar car pulled up in front of Matt's house. Marshall stepped out of the passenger side. From the driver's side emerged a heavy-set man that Matt assumed to be Captain Drake.

Once inside, Marshall introduced Drake to Matt, who was favorably impressed. *He even looks like a detective,* Matt thought, noticing Drake's steely gray eyes and prematurely gray hair. After they shook hands, Matt thanked Drake for going out of his way to facilitate the search for Priscilla. "I realize you usually wait twenty-four hours before initiating any action in these cases," he said.

"I'm glad to help," said Drake. "I happen to think a lot of this man." He nodded toward Marshall. "Any time he needs my help, he's got it. You should understand, though, that there are reasons we don't ordinarily take missing person reports before twenty-four hours elapse, or even forty-eight hours.

"First, it's not against the law to be missing. Sometimes people want to be missing, for any number of reasons, and that's their right. Usually they show up within a day or two.

"However, if we have reason to suspect foul play, we don't wait twenty-four hours to act. Of course, it also depends on our case load. I have only one detective working full time on missing persons, and there's a limit to what he can do. So this one's on me."

"I understand," said Matt, "and I really appreciate it. As far as Priscilla is concerned, I don't know what to think. It's not like her at all to just disappear without telling anyone. She knows we'd all be worried sick about her, and she just wouldn't do anything so cruel and irresponsible."

Marshall nodded vigorously in agreement, and Matt continued, "On the other hand, I can't think of a soul who'd want to hurt Priscilla, either. And I certainly don't have the kind of money that someone would grab her for ransom."

"Sir, I understand you have had some recent problems between the two of you," said Drake. "Could it be that she wanted to get away from that situation for a while?"

"No way," said Matt, "not without telling me. Not without telling somebody. Besides that, she didn't take anything with her but the clothes on her back. I checked."

"Yes, sir. And when did you last see or talk with Mrs. Douglas, sir?"

"Yesterday morning when she left for school," said Matt, trying not to sound irritated and wondering what this sudden "sir" business from Drake meant.

"How would you characterize her mood at the time?" asked Drake. "Did she say or do anything you would consider unusual?"

"No, she didn't. Okay, look, things were a bit cool between us and neither one of us said much, but there was nothing that would remotely explain her disappearance. Nothing!"

"You say you haven't seen or talked with Mrs. Douglas since yesterday morning. The secretary at McKinley School"—he paused and looked at his notebook—"a Mrs. Betty Dugan, says you called for Mrs. Douglas at noon and asked that she return your call. Mrs. Dugan says she gave Mrs. Douglas your message and that she personally saw her then go to the telephone. Now, sir, are you sure you didn't talk with your wife yesterday during the noon hour?"

"I'm sure," said Matt.

"Well, sir, who do you think she would have called when the secretary gave her a message to call you?"

"I don't know," said Matt. "Maybe she did try to call me. Maybe the line was busy." He shifted nervously from one foot to the other and glanced at Marshall, who seemed to be hanging on every word.

"Maybe," said Drake. "Marshall tells me you came to his place looking for Mrs. Douglas at about eight o'clock last night. What time do you ordinarily get home from work, Mr. Douglas?"

"It varies," said Matt. "Usually between six and six-thirty."

"And was that the time you arrived home last night?"

"Yes, yes, it was about that time. Wait. No, I—uh—" Suddenly Matt remembered he had left work a little early and hurried home to invite Priscilla to dinner at the Rhinelander. He began to perspire. "I guess I got home a little earlier last night—maybe five-fifteen or five-thirty."

"And from the time you got home, at maybe five-fifteen, until you arrived at Marshall's house about eight, can you account for your time and whereabouts?"

"What is this?" said Matt, no longer able to conceal his irritation. "Am I a suspect in my own wife's disappearance?"

"Just routine questions, Mr. Douglas," said Drake. "The time between five-fifteen and eight last night?"

"I was at home waiting for Priscilla."

"Alone, I presume."

"Yes, alone." Matt felt guilty even though he knew he was innocent. How humiliating to be suspected like this! He hardly dared look at Marshall again. What in the world must he think?

"Just one or two more questions," Drake continued. "Concerning this man Profett. I understand that Mrs. Douglas didn't like him. May I assume those feelings were mutual?"

"Actually, you can't." Matt's mind raced. He wanted to jump all over Drake for insensitively referring to Priscilla in the past tense, but he thought better of it. "Mr. Profett does not like women in general, but he has no reason to dislike Priscilla in particular. He hasn't even met her."

"Okay, just one more thing. Have you had any communication of any kind with Robert Pressler?"

"Who?" said Matt. "I've never even heard of any Robert Pressler."

"Yes, you have," Marshall interjected. "Don't you remember? He's the busboy at the Prime Cut, the one with the long criminal record."

"Oh, him," said Matt. "No, of course I haven't had any contact with him. Why would I? What has he got to do with any of this?"

"Probably nothing," said Drake. "But it's possible the maitre d' mentioned your paying twenty dollars for a drinking glass from a table he had bussed. Some of these losers are pretty paranoid, sir. He might have thought you were trying to get the goods on him. If so—"

Matt sighed heavily. What a nightmare this was becoming!

Mercifully, Drake cut the interview short. "You've been most helpful, and I want to thank you for your cooperation." He sounded like a recording, and Matt knew he'd said the same words to a hundred suspects in a hundred different cases.

Matt said his goodbyes to Marshall and Captain Drake as they headed out the door, and turned wearily back into the screaming loneliness and emptiness of his house.

The next thing he had to do was face Diane and David and tell them their mother was missing. How could he do that? For the first time tears filled his eyes. They blurred his vision and made it hard for him to see. He dropped heavily onto the sofa, buried his head in his hands, and sobbed out his grief. "Oh, God," he said over and over. "Oh, God."

11

Just before ten, Matt saw Profett's car turn into his driveway. He had mixed feelings about the man being here. Ordinarily he would have much preferred to handle family matters within the family. However, this was no ordinary situation, and John Profett was no ordinary acquaintance. The man *had* prayed all night for them.

Matt was having difficulty believing Profett's assurance that Priscilla was all right, but it was certainly the most—and only—encouraging thing he had to go on so far.

Profett jumped out of his car and walked quickly to the front door Matt held open. "Come in," Matt said, "it's nasty out there."

"No word yet?" Profett asked, searching Matt's face.

"No," said Matt. He returned Profett's gaze and was surprised to see tears in the man's eyes and a drawn look on his face. Matt knew he himself must look a mess, but he hadn't expected Profett to be affected so deeply.

Matt's own tears flowed again as Profett threw his arms awkwardly around him and held him in a tight hug. "She's going to be okay, Matt," he said. "Thank God, she's going to be okay."

The two men went into the kitchen, and Profett said, "Look, I'm here to help however you need me. I can man the phone, make calls, run errands, or just stand by for whatever develops. What do you think, Matt? How can I help the most?"

"Probably just by being here in case Priscilla—or anyone—calls,"

CHAPTER ELEVEN * 65

said Matt. "I hate to be away from the phone even briefly myself, but I've got to see David and Diane. I can't tell them something like this over the phone, and I can't send someone else to tell them either.

"I won't be gone any longer than I absolutely must," Matt continued. "I'll pick up David at Multnomah, then he and I will drive to Newberg and tell Diane. They'll probably both come home with me. I'll call you from Newberg, just to check in."

Matt washed up and shaved. He didn't want his appearance to alarm the kids more than his news itself would. He showed Profett around the house, told him to make himself at home, and left.

Profett watched as Matt's car rounded the corner and drove out of sight. He checked his watch: almost ten-thirty. He settled at the table and browsed through the *Oregonian* for fifteen minutes. Matt would have been back by now if he were returning for something he had forgotten. Profett took out his wallet and unfolded a scrap of paper. He picked up the phone, dialed the number written on the paper, and waited.

"Yeah," a voice finally said on the other end of the line. "Whatcha want?"

"This is Matt Douglas," said Profett, "calling about that little lesson I asked you to teach my wife. Everything's going according to plan on this end. How are things there?"

"Not a hitch," answered the shorter of Priscilla's two kidnappers. "Her car brought us a nice piece of change from the chop shop, and we have truly enjoyed the pleasure of her company." He laughed. "Call on us any time you need work done."

"Let's finish this job, first," said Profett. "It's crucially important you say exactly the right thing when you call here with your ransom demands. Have you got the script I wrote for you?"

"We've got it, and we've practiced it. Relax, will you? You'll get what you bargained for."

Profett hung up the phone. "Now let's see," he murmured, "I might as well do something useful while I'm waiting for their call." He walked down the hall to Matt and Priscilla's bedroom. There on her nightstand he found Priscilla's daily journal. He opened it, flopped on the bed, and began reading.

✳   ✳   ✳

Across town, the journal's owner lay disconsolate on some old blankets in the corner of an upstairs room. Her clothes were torn and in disarray. An ugly bruise had swollen her left eye half closed.

They had raped her last night. Both of them. She had resisted at first, and that was when the shorter one, the driver, who also seemed to be the leader, had hit her, hard, with his fist.

"I don't need you conscious," he had told her after striking her. "It's all up to you how rough I get."

From that point on, she had been totally passive, trying not even to be there as first the driver and then the man with crooked teeth abused her.

She had little doubt what they would do next. Poor Matt and David and Diane. They would be devastated at losing her so suddenly. Glimpses of her memorial service came before her mind, and she could see her family weeping at the casket. Her dad would be inconsolable, too. How much she loved each of them! How much they had loved her! And now it was all so quickly shattered and gone. These brutes might keep her here a few more hours, or maybe even days, to use and abuse her, but in the end they would surely kill her.

✳   ✳   ✳

Diane Douglas was surprised to hear her dad's voice on the house phone in her residence at Marshall Fox College. What was he doing in Newberg on a Saturday?

When Diane reached the lounge and saw her brother David with her dad, her curiosity took an anxious turn. Her father looked strange. Was he ill?

"What is it, Dad? What's wrong?" she asked.

"I don't want you to imagine the worst," Matt said. "We don't really know that anything bad has happened, but—it's your mother; she's been missing since last night."

"Missing?" said Diane, looking first at Matt and then at David for some explanation. "But—but where could she be? I mean, how can she be missing? You mean you *don't* know where she is?"

"She didn't come home from school yesterday," said Matt. "That's all we know." Matt took Diane in his arms. "I need you and David at home with me until we find her. Grab whatever you need for a couple of days, and let's go."

While Diane was gathering a few things from her room, Matt went to the phone and dialed his home number. When there was no answer, he decided he must have misdialed; Profett had to be there. He dialed again carefully and let it ring ten times, fifteen, twenty.

What is this? Matt thought. *Doesn't anything work right anymore? I must be in the Twilight Zone.*

As they drove toward home, Matt told Diane and David everything he knew about their mother's disappearance, including the latest disquieting development. Profett, who was holding the fort at home, was not answering the phone. Either the phone was out of order, or something had happened to Profett.

"If we don't see Profett's car at the house," Matt said, "something's up."

As they rode along, Diane bowed her head and prayed. She prayed first for her father, who was under tremendous strain. She prayed for David, bravely trying to conceal his fear. Most of all, she prayed for her mother, that God would be with her and bring her safely home.

As they rounded the last corner before the house, three pairs of eyes searched in vain for Profett's car. Matt parked in the empty driveway, and they all went inside.

The house was so hollow, it seemed spooky to Diane. She had spent her growing years here—the only place she had known as home. Although nothing about the place had changed physically, now everything seemed different. Her mother was gone. She fought to hold back tears as her eyes filled, but one tear escaped to roll slowly down her cheek.

They looked for a note Profett might have left to explain his departure. There was nothing.

"Now what?" said David, looking to his father for direction.

Diane saw her father's face sag; he seemed to have aged ten years. "I don't know," he said.

Instinctively the three of them huddled in an embrace. "Oh, Lord," Matt began to pray, but he could not continue. "Oh, Lord," he began again after a long pause, "our hope is in you; we need you." Diane felt his body shake, and together the three of them gave way to their grief.

* * *

Priscilla had already resigned herself to her fate. Whatever these animals did to her now couldn't matter—soon she would be away from them and with Christ. Still, she trembled when she heard sounds of someone approaching in the hall.

The door opened and there stood the tall one with the crooked teeth. "We're getting sick and tired of you," he said. "It's time we unloaded you; come on." He grabbed her by the arm, half dragged her downstairs, and shoved her onto a torn old sofa in the front room. The driver sat at the kitchen table, where the contents of her purse were strewn.

"Okay, Priscilla Douglas, wife of Matthew Douglas," said the driver, "let's see if old Matthew wants you back." He was holding her checkbook with their address and phone number.

He dialed the number. When the telephone rang at the Douglas home, John Profett waited until the answering machine turned on, then picked up the receiver and said, "Douglas residence."

"Hey, Douglas," said the driver. "You been wonderin' what happened to the little lady, have you?"

"Who is this?" Profett demanded.

"We're friends of Mrs. Douglas," said the driver. "Brand new friends." He laughed. "She's had a little car trouble. You know? We want to give her a ride home, but gas is expensive. We wondered if you'd be willing to pay for our gas and maybe a little somethin' for our time and trouble."

"Of course," said Profett, "but why don't I just come and get her. Let me speak with her, please."

"Oh, you can't come and get her," said the driver. "This is kind of a bad neighborhood. You know? We couldn't take a chance of you comin' down here. Somethin' could happen to you." He laughed again. "Probably would!"

"I'll take that risk," said Profett evenly. "But how do I know she's even there? Let me speak with her."

"Okay," said the voice, "you can talk to her, 'cause you better know we ain't foolin."

"Matt!" cried a woman's voice in the background. "Please, Matt, do what they say. I—"

"Now, look, Douglas," the driver broke in. "Ten thousand dollars will get you your lady back. Or ain't you that fond of her?"

"Now, you look," said Profett, shouting angrily. "That woman you're holding is under God's protection. Lay a hand on her, and you'll regret it, I promise you. I'm not going to pay you one dime, but if you let her go, I'll spare your miserable life. Let her go!" he repeated, and then he literally roared, "NOW!"

Priscilla watched with amazement at the strange sequence of events that followed. The driver dropped the phone and grabbed his accomplice by the arm. "Hey, man, we got trouble," he said, his eyes wide with fright. "Look!"

Priscilla followed his gaze out the front window and saw nothing. However, when the man with the crooked teeth looked, he gasped and acted like he'd seen death in person. "There's too many of 'em," he croaked. "Run for it!"

At that both men dashed toward the back of the house, and Priscilla heard a door slam. Then she was alone in the silence. Hesitantly, she picked up the phone. "Hello," she said in a hoarse whisper. "Matt, is that you?"

"Priscilla? This is John Profett. What's happening there?"

"I don't know," whispered Priscilla. "He suddenly dropped the phone and both of them went running out the back."

"Quickly!" said Profett. "Tell me where you are and I'll come for you."

"I don't know!" wailed Priscilla.

"Keep calm," ordered Profett. "Is there a window in that room?"

"Yes."

"Go to the window, look out, and see if you can see anything to identify your location."

"There's a big old black car in front of the house across the street. Both front wheels are off," said Priscilla.

"Good!" said Profett. "What else? What does the house across the street look like? Can you see a number?"

"The house is green," said Priscilla, "an ugly faded green, and the number looks like 3819—or maybe it's 3879. Oh, I can't tell what it is," she cried shakily.

"That's okay," said Profett. "Close enough. Now, what street is it? Are you near enough to a corner to see a street sign anywhere?"

"No, I can't," said Priscilla. "We're in the middle of the block." She heard a sound from somewhere in the house and let out an involuntary gasp, "Uhhhnnn, I think they're coming back!"

"Keep calm! When they took you there, did you see anything that would help you identify the area?"

"No, I was too upset. I—I—wait! We were going out Martin Luther King Jr. Boulevard and then we turned right and went about two blocks. That would make this Sixth Street, I think, or Seventh."

"Great!" said Profett. "I'll be there just as quick as I can drive it."

"But I think they're still here," whispered Priscilla. "I—I hear them."

"God is going to deliver you," said Profett. "Just hold on."

Twenty minutes later, John Profett swept down the 3800 block of Northeast Sixth Street and spotted the derelict car and the green house. He swerved to the left and parked on the wrong side of the street, then jumped out and walked boldly to the front door.

He pounded on the door and shouted, "Open up!" When there was no response, he turned the knob and flung open the door. He marched in and called Priscilla's name. There was no reply.

"Priscilla!" he shouted again. "Where are you?"

Just off the entry to the left was a room with the door closed. He threw it open and saw a table littered with the contents of an emptied purse, but no one was there. He proceeded through the house looking into each room until he reached the open back door. Priscilla was nowhere to be found.

He returned through the house to the front door and started up the staircase there. At the top was a hall with rooms on each side. He flung open the door to the rooms one by one. Finally, in the farthest corner of the last room, he saw the huddled figure of a woman on the floor. "Priscilla," he said, "I'm John Profett. I've come to take you home."

12

Priscilla, escorted by Profett, approached the front door of the Douglas home when suddenly it flew open and Matt, Diane and David rushed out to meet her. Tears flowed with their embraces, and each of them embraced Profett too, although Diane and David were meeting him for the first time.

Profett had called from the hospital to tell Matt that he was bringing Priscilla home, that she had been raped, that except for a black eye, she seemed to be okay physically. He also told Matt that his entire conversation with the kidnappers was recorded on the phone answering machine, and that he should preserve the recording for evidence.

Now Profett knew it was time to leave the Douglas family alone. "I'll check back with you tomorrow," he said, standing in the entry and declining Matt's invitation to come in for even a few minutes. "Right now, you need privacy and rest." He turned to Diane and David. "And you two will see that they get it, won't you?"

"We certainly will," said Diane, "and, again, we can't tell you how grateful we are for all you've done."

Matt walked Profett back out to his car. Once there, he grasped Profett's hand, shaking it warmly. "Thanks," he said, "I'm in your debt forever." He lowered his voice. "About the rape, I'd just as soon you didn't mention it to anyone, at least until we decide how we're going to deal with it."

"Of course," said Profett, clapping Matt on the shoulder. "I understand perfectly."

Then Profett was gone. Back inside, Matt found Priscilla with David and Diane hovering around her in the kitchen. She straightened up the tabletop, then gathered several sections of newspaper and placed them in the recycling bag she kept next to the refrigerator. A couple of coffee cups were in the sink, and she put them in the dishwasher.

"I'll take care of those things, Mother!" said Diane, looking to her father to back her up.

Matt swept Priscilla up in his arms. "You are going to rest," he stated flatly. "Now, come on."

Priscilla allowed Matt to lead her into the bedroom, where she smoothed the rumpled bedspread before turning down the covers.

"Sleep as long as you can," Matt said. "When you get up, if you feel like it, we'll have dinner."

Priscilla walked into the master bath, locked the door, and turned on the shower. Matt returned to the kitchen, where he found David and Diane arguing. "What's the problem?" he asked.

"Oh, nothing," Diane said. "How's Mother? Is she okay?"

"Oh, sure," said Matt. "She's showering now, and then a few hours' sleep will work wonders for her."

Diane nodded. "Speaking of which, you could stand some sleep yourself, Dad."

"You're right," said Matt without a hint of protest. "A couple of hours will work wonders for me, too. And then, I told your mother we could all have dinner together this evening. I think there are some steaks in the freezer; want to get them out?"

Diane nodded and started trolling through the fridge. "Here's peas and corn, and I'll see what I can find for dessert."

Matt headed for the bedroom, and as soon as he was gone, Diane turned to David. "See, I told you he was exhausted. What good would it do anyhow? Going over there is a hare-brained idea."

"I wish Rick was here," said David, missing his old high-school buddy. "He'd go with me in a minute."

"Yes," said Diane, "because he's just as crazy as you are. Or more so." Her voice softened a little. "How's old Rick doing in the army anyhow? I'm surprised he hasn't washed out by now."

"He's doing great," said David. "Every time he writes, he tells me what a mistake I made by not enlisting with him."

"Oh, yeah, big mistake!" said Diane. "Going to Multnomah was one of the few things you've done right."

"I'm calling Grandpa," said David, picking up the phone. "I bet he'll go with me."

Matt had called Marshall with the news of Priscilla's rescue and Marshall's first inclination had been to rush over to see her, but he'd thought better of it. Now, however, he was intrigued by David's suggestion—that they drive to the northeast Portland house where, as the telephone tape revealed, Priscilla had been held. He was intrigued, but also cautious.

"And do what?" he asked.

"I don't know," said David. "Maybe we'll find some evidence the cops could use, something to help nail those rats."

"And maybe the 'rats' will be there," said Marshall. "Have you thought about that? They are no doubt armed and dangerous. In fact, just going to that area could be risky."

"I'll take my gun," said David, referring to his 9mm Luger Marshall had given him on his eighteenth birthday. The Luger, Marshall had explained at the time, was just like the first gun he had owned and the one he had taught David's mother to use when she was his age.

Now David was feeling invincible because of the gun. "I hope they are there and try something," he said; "I'll shoot them down like the rats they are."

"Or they'll shoot you," said Marshall. "How do you think that would make your mother feel?" He paused. "I'll go with you, David, but I want us to go prepared, okay? And I don't mean armed. I have a friend who's a policeman; he's already involved in this case. Let me call him and then I'll call you back."

David hung up the phone and turned to face Diane, whose concern clearly showed on her face. "He's going with me," said David, "and so's his friend who's a cop."

Diane raised her eyebrows but also breathed a sigh of relief to hear that a couple of trustworthy adults would be riding herd on her little brother, who wasn't known for good judgment even in normal times.

"Let me know when Grandpa calls," said David, "I'll be in my room."

David went to his room and took his pistol from underneath the paint-stained sweatshirt in the third drawer of his chest. From the very back of his writing-desk drawer, he fished out a box of long rifle magnum shells. He filled the magazine of the nine-shot repeater, then dumped as many more bullets into his left pants pocket. He dug a bulky old army surplus jacket out of his closet. It had a deep vest pocket, perfect for carrying the gun.

"David," he heard Diane call. "Telephone—it's Grandpa."

Meanwhile, in the master bedroom, Matt was standing at the bathroom door knocking. "Priscilla," he called. "Priscilla, please unlock the door."

Priscilla had always been the speed shower champion of the Douglas family. When the kids were young, she could take her shower as well as bathe and dress both kids in the time it took Matt to clean up and dress for church or whatever. Two minutes was about as long as she ever stayed in the shower, but now she had been in there so long with the water running that Matt was getting worried.

Finally the door opened to his insistent knock, and Matt entered a steam room. Water had condensed on the mirror until it was running down in little rivulets. Puddles sat on the window sill, and even the tiny flocked daisies on the wallpaper were soggy, despite the ceiling exhaust fan's futile efforts to pump out the excess moisture. Priscilla stood there wrapped in a huge bath towel, shivering. "I ran out of hot water," she said.

"Come on, honey," said Matt. "The electric blanket is on and the bed's all nice and warm."

She pulled her long flannel nightgown on over her head and crawled into bed as Matt stood by awkwardly. He then made a gesture toward tucking her in, kissed her on the cheek, walked around to the other side of their double king-size bed, and settled in for a nap. Their bed was plenty big enough for each of them to stretch out without touching the other.

In moments, both were sound asleep.

*   *   *

Less than one hour after he had called David, Marshall arrived with Captain Drake in an unmarked police car at the Douglas home. David pulled on his heavy jacket made heavier by the weight of the Luger and stepped out the front door.

*   *   *

"No! No! Get away from me!" Priscilla yelled as she fought and scratched. She struggled against the firm grip on both arms, saw the leering crooked-toothed face, smelled the boozy breath.

Matt was holding her, shaking her, speaking to her loudly. "Priscilla! Wake up! Wake up!"

Gradually, the light of recognition came into her eyes. "What—" she began. "Unnhhh," she let out a long sobbing sigh as the reality of being at home in bed with her husband replaced the horror of assault. "Oh, Matt!" she moaned.

Both of them were sitting up now, and he took her in his arms. "It's all right," he said. "Everything's all right. You were having a bad dream."

She endured his embrace briefly, though his touch made her sick to her stomach. It wasn't Matt's fault, and she didn't want to hurt his feelings, but she finally pulled away.

"Do you want to talk about it?" asked Matt.

Priscilla did not answer but began to cry.

He desperately wanted to help somehow, but she obviously didn't want him to hold her. "Did you dream about—about it?" he probed gently.

She nodded, and after a few moments said slowly, "I don't know if I can make it, Matt."

"Of course you can make it," he said. "You're unsinkable."

He comforted her for a few more moments and got her to lie down again. He lay there beside her until her regular breathing told him she was asleep. Then he quietly got up, dressed, and went out to the kitchen with Diane.

"Dad, you didn't sleep long," Diane said.

"No, your mother had a nightmare and woke us both up. I finally got her to sleep again though."

"I'm worried about her," said Diane. "Do you really think she's going to be all right?"

"Your mother is one strong woman," said Matt. "She'll be all right. Why do you think I've always called her 'the unsinkable 'Scilla Brown'?"

"I don't know," said Diane. "I know you call her that once in a while, but I never really understood why."

"Then let me tell you the story," said Matt, sitting down in a kitchen chair. "It traces back to before we were married, before we even started dating. Your mother was going with a friend of mine named Clint. Though I was attracted to this Priscilla of his, there was no way I was going to muscle in on my friend.

"Then Claudia, who was your mother's best friend at the time, kind of cornered me at church one day and asked me if I liked Priscilla. When I admitted that I did, she told me that I should ask her out. I said I couldn't because, while I liked Priscilla, I loved Clint."

"Wait," said Diane. "You mean her best friend wanted you to date Mother? She must have known Mother liked you."

"Not quite," said Matt. "During summer vacation, while your mother was away working as a camp counselor, Claudia started dating Clint. Then I understood why she had tried to pair me up with Priscilla; she wanted Clint. By fall, when your mother was back on the scene again, Clint and Claudia were practically engaged."

"Oh, no!" said Diane. "Poor Mother, losing her boyfriend and being betrayed by her best friend like that. She must have been devastated."

"Yes," said Matt, "but obviously it all worked out for the best—or she'd never have gotten me!"

"Oh, obviously," agreed Diane, grinning. "But I thought you were going to tell me how you came to call mother 'the unsinkable 'Scilla Brown.' "

"Well," said Matt, "there was an immensely popular play back then called *The Unsinkable Molly Brown,* and it had been made into a movie starring Debbie Reynolds. It was about a young woman with big dreams who accidentally burned up her first $300,000 fortune in her wood stove before eventually becoming a heroine in the sinking of the *Titanic.*

"Your mother remarked to me one day that I didn't need to worry about her getting over Clint and Claudia because she was 'the unsinkable 'Scilla Brown.' I've called her that ever since, whenever she shows strength in the face of adversity."

"That's a great story," said Diane. She walked over to the chair where he was sitting and took his hand. "Thanks, Dad, for telling me; it makes me proud of both of you."

"Both of us?" echoed Matt. "What did I do?"

"You told that conniving Claudia that you *liked* her friend but you *loved* your friend. That was beautiful, Dad. And I'd say that those two deserved each other."

Diane went back to work in the kitchen, singing a happy song.

*   *   *

Instead of going directly to northeast Portland, "Captain Drake" swung by the East Precinct of the Portland Police Bureau on 47th and Burnside. "Come on into my office for a minute," he told Marshall and David. "We need to talk about something before we go on."

Drake led the two through the outer office and down a corridor. He unlocked a door that said "Captain Rodney Drake" on it in gold letters, then stood there motioning for the other two to enter ahead of him.

Marshall passed through into the office, and as David followed he suddenly felt a strong arm seize him around the neck from behind. In a moment, Drake's other hand had reached inside

David's jacket and pulled out his pistol.

"What—what's the big idea?" sputtered David.

"Carrying a concealed weapon is against the law, young man," Drake said. "Unless, of course, you have a permit. Do you?"

David hung his head and murmured an almost inaudible no.

"I can't hear you," said Drake. "Have you got a permit to carry this gun or haven't you?"

"I haven't," said David, looking into Drake's frowning face and then looking forlornly at his grandfather.

"You have to decide," said Drake, his face about one inch from David's and his eyes blazing, "which side of the law you are going to be on. Like I had to decide. Like your grandfather here had to decide. Like those vermin who kidnapped your mother had to decide. Only we decided to respect the law, and they couldn't care less. Right now you look more like them than like us. Is that what you want?"

"No."

"Okay," said Drake, removing the magazine from David's gun and handing it to him. "Put that in your pocket. We'll leave the gun here on my desk and pick it up on our way home. Now let's go check out that house."

13

"CARJACKING KIDNAP VICTIM RESCUED"

So read the Sunday newspaper.

"A Beaverton woman kidnapped Friday in a carjacking near Lloyd Center was rescued Saturday by a Colton man . . ."

Toward the end, the article mentioned that the rescuer, John Profett, had written a bestselling book—*1999*—and was considered by some to be a modern prophet.

By afternoon, the Douglas home had become a busy gathering place of friends, neighbors and relatives. Early, before most of them started coming, Marshall Brown had taken the opportunity to talk alone with Matt about Profett.

"The guy has come out looking like quite a hero," said Marshall, "but I don't trust him. I'd be very careful about teaming up with him, if I were you."

"I am being careful," said Matt.

"Has it occurred to you—?" Marshall hesitated, though it was clear he had more on his mind.

"What?" said Matt. "Go ahead and say it."

"Has it occurred to you that Profett might possibly be mixed up in the abduction of Priscilla?"

Matt nodded. He decided not to crow about being way ahead of Marshall, so he simply said quietly, "I have thought of that, and I've concluded it's not plausible."

"Why not?" asked Marshall.

"Well, for at least a couple of reasons. First, he'd need a motive, and he hasn't got one that I can think of.

"Second, and more important, it just doesn't add up. This is a man of God we're talking about. He is obviously at home and accepted among Christians in a way he could not be without having had a long-time association with the church. He's also a serious student of the Bible."

"But even preachers fall," said Marshall, "and they can do some pretty terrible things."

"Yes, they can," Matt agreed. "I know that Profett, or anyone else, might fall. But do this to Priscilla? This was not the work of a good man fallen. Profett would have to be evil—and I mean totally ruthless—to have done this. That simply doesn't fit the man I see."

Reluctantly, Marshall had to acknowledge Matt's point. "Maybe you're right," he said, "but that doesn't mean you should join him."

"No, but there's no reason I shouldn't either. Actually, this whole episode gives me more reason than ever to join Profett."

"More reason?" asked Marshall. "How do you figure that?"

"Well, look at it this way," said Matt. "Something's going on here. Either this is the start of something big—and I mean something really great—for God, or Profett's one of the biggest frauds ever to come along. I intend to find out which it is. And the extremely unlikely possibility that Profett may be implicated in the attack on Priscilla only makes my involvement more necessary. Because if he was in on that, I'm going to nail him."

Later in the day as more and more people stopped in, and especially after John Profett arrived, a near-festive mood prevailed in the Douglas home. Each new group prompted a fresh telling of the story.

Matt never seemed to tire of describing how he had been almost out of his mind with worry. Profett had been the one to offer him hope when he had no reason to hope. Profett had come to his home without being asked. Profett had kept watch while Matt went to tell David and Diane the crushing news. Profett had masterfully handled the crisis when the phone call came demanding money for Priscilla's release.

Profett had figured out where Priscilla was and had fearlessly gone there and rescued her.

Even Captain Drake stopped in briefly mid-afternoon to join in the celebration and to congratulate the Douglas family. In retelling the story this time, Matt included more detail about Drake's role. "I was even a suspect for a while," he said with a laugh. "This officer doesn't trust anyone! I have to admit, I was offended at the time. But I'm not mad any more. Today I'm not mad at anybody. I'm just so grateful to God. And to John Profett!"

Drake, for his part, was careful to frown officially on Profett's private rescue operation. "People should call the police and not try to deal with criminals on their own," he said. "It certainly was a gutsy thing to do, though," he added, betraying a grudging admiration.

Profett, all the while, modestly declined to say much, preferring simply to soak up the praise and the admiring glances of the others.

Priscilla stayed in bed in her room most of the day. People understood, considering the trauma she had endured. "Just imagine!" they commented to one another. A couple of especially close friends—Jill Farmsly from across the street and Donna Crowley from church—stepped into her room to assure Priscilla of their love and prayers, but no one pressed for any details.

Matt supplied a bare bones explanation of what had happened so that people wouldn't be left to wonder and to speculate. He didn't mention the rape. Why humiliate Priscilla further by letting the whole world know everything that had happened? Privacy was important at a time like this. So far, he and Priscilla hadn't even told Diane and David, or Marshall, and it was probably best left that way.

The main thing to say was that Priscilla had been kidnapped and assaulted, but God had heard all their prayers for her safe return. Particularly, as it now appeared, he had heard Profett's night-long prayers on her behalf.

Incredibly, the kidnappers had quaked at the voice of John Profett on the phone, and had run in panic before he even went to the house. Priscilla had reported what her captors said about seeing a force that was "too many" for them, and everyone seemed to agree that God had sent a band of angels to rescue her.

Profett dismissed his own part in producing such fear. " 'The wicked man flees though no one pursues,' " he said. "Proverbs 28:1." Someone reminded the others about the last half of the verse, which Profett had modestly omitted: "But the righteous are as bold as a lion." Everyone murmured agreement to those words, but Profett just looked down, then said, "To God be the glory."

Perhaps the best explanation for the entire incident, from a natural viewpoint, was Captain Drake's. He surmised it had been a "crime of opportunity."

"Priscilla just happened to be in the wrong place at the wrong time," he said. "Her abduction could not have been planned because no one even knew she would be there.

"She was quite insistent about that," continued Drake. "She told us that she didn't know she was going to the Lloyd Center until the moment she turned right on McLoughlin. The perpetrators were probably cruising the area, looking for an easy mark, a vulnerable person driving a desirable car. We've been getting those kinds of crimes lately. Unfortunately, Priscilla supplied exactly what they were looking for."

Throughout the afternoon Profett virtually held court at the Douglas home. Some people, like Priscilla and her father, had been hostile—or at best skeptical—toward him. To the degree they were not now totally won over, they were at least silenced. How could they oppose someone who had done so much for them?

Though Priscilla hardly talked with any visitors during the day, she did make it clear to Matt that her former opposition to Profett had melted like yesterday's snow in the west hills.

Marshall expressed his heartfelt, if uncertain, appreciation to Profett for the rescue of his daughter. "Besides saving Priscilla, you have saved my trip to Eastern Europe," he said. Marshall explained that he had planned an extended visit to Romania, Hungary and Ukraine to scout investment opportunities there for clients of JBC Investments.

He was scheduled to leave that coming week, but when Priscilla disappeared, those plans were put on hold. He obviously couldn't leave not knowing what had happened to Priscilla. But now he could go knowing that all was well.

"I'm indebted to you," Marshall told Profett, "and if there's anything I can do for you, here or in Eastern Europe, I'd be more than happy to do it."

"Thank you so much for that kind offer," said Profett. "Anything you feel led to do to spread the message of our Lord's imminent return will be much appreciated."

Marshall decided not to get into the issue of their divergent views on prophecy. He didn't need to agree with Profett in order to be of service to him. He ended up committing to air express one hundred copies of *1999* to each country, and to distribute them to key people.

Larry Forrester was another admirer come to pay tribute to Profett that wonderful afternoon. This time it was Diane's turn to describe to Larry and the room full of people the events of the previous day.

"You can't believe how devastating it was when we came home with Mother missing and found that Mr. Profett had vanished too. Fortunately, we weren't left in that terrible confusion very long. About twenty minutes after we walked in the door, the phone rang. It was Mr. Profett calling from the hospital to tell us Mother was shaken and traumatized but okay, and they were on their way home."

Larry listened to her story with starry eyes. He admired Christian leaders generally, and he practically idolized Profett because of *1999*. Now the man was also a Douglas family personal hero for rescuing Diane's mother.

Diane sat Larry down near Profett, introducing him as her special friend and a football star from Portland State. She also mentioned his unchurched background. Profett treated Larry as if he were someone really important. He showed great interest when Larry mentioned that he hoped to become a pastor someday. "God is looking for men who have the courage to stand without compromise for him," said Profett. "Standing alone in your family is something I greatly admire."

Later, when it was time for Larry to leave, Diane went too, accepting a ride back to Newberg with him. All the way, they talked of only one thing. Priscilla had whispered it to Diane in a private moment that afternoon. John Profett was more than a man of God, more than a hero. He was the person prophesied to come in the closing verses of the Old Testament: *Elijah.*

"And to think, we actually know him!" marveled Larry. "Did you hear what he said to me? He said—I can't believe it—he said that *he admires me!*"

Meanwhile, with the last of their guests and John Profett gone home, Priscilla came out into the living room for a little while. Matt gently took her in his arms. "Well, 'Scill," he said, "this has been quite a ride, but we made it. And, you know, bad as this whole thing was, God is bringing good out of it. I can't tell you how much it means to have you with me on this Profett thing." He paused. "Quite a guy, isn't he?"

"I'll say!" agreed Priscilla. She looked up into Matt's face. "When I'm wrong, I'm really wrong, huh?"

He simply hugged her tighter in reply, and she continued. "But you won't have to worry about me any more. I've learned my lesson."

"That's great," said Matt. "And, you know, I think John and I have learned something too. I think we both realize better now that when he hires me, he gets a package. Not just Matt Douglas but Matt who's married to Priscilla.

"And guess what," Matt continued, his eyes asparkle.

"What?" said Priscilla.

"John says the next thing he wants to do is sit down and talk with both of us about what the Lord has in store for us from here on out. He made it clear he wants you at our next meeting," said Matt. "What do you think of that?"

"It's wonderful," said Priscilla, tears in her eyes. "After all I've put everyone through, I'm surprised he'd want me anywhere near him."

Matt turned her face up toward his and kissed her on the lips. "I'm not surprised," he said. "The man wouldn't be much of a prophet if he couldn't see how special you are."

14

For Matt the issue of John Profett was now largely decided. Intellectually, he could crank out all kinds of questions about Profett's claim to be Elijah. In the back of his mind, he also filed away a few lingering doubts about the man's integrity. However, emotionally he felt John Profett was clearly God's man.

Matt had also discovered more and more Scripture that supported the belief in an end-time ministry for Elijah. He couldn't wait to stimulate some pointed discussions of these passages among Christian leaders, and to participate in such discussions himself.

These feelings caused Matt to anticipate the Monday and Tuesday editions of "Hear and Now" more keenly than ever. The scheduled discussions—about whether the Elijah prophecy should be taken literally—were now monumental in importance. They could provide an enormous leap forward on this incredible journey leading to the return of Jesus Christ.

Matt had produced some teases for his Monday and Tuesday programs. KOCB had aired them heavily toward the end of last week and over the weekend:

Will the prophet Elijah return before Christ comes? How are we to understand the last verses of the Old Testament, which tell us that he will? Could Elijah already be among us? Don't miss "Elijah—Shall We Expect Him?" a special two-part "Hear and Now" program Monday and Tuesday right here on KOCB, the voice of Oregon Christian Broadcasting.

Matt had already talked with Dr. Jim Zander and Dr. Elaine Newman, his guests, to learn their general views on the prophecy. He knew Dr. Zander would argue against expecting Elijah to return, while Dr. Newman would speak in favor of that expectation.

When he first scheduled them, Matt himself had been undecided and wanted to hear both sides. Now he was tempted to tell Dr. Zander to stay home, and in his place to schedule someone who would be more supportive of the truth as he had come to believe it.

Matt thought better of that idea for two reasons. First, he was a professional, and he had to maintain a professional impartiality regardless of his personal views.

Second, and perhaps more important, people needed to hear both sides so that their convictions would be firmly based. To Matt, the emerging evidence for an Elijah role in Christ's return was becoming so strong that the opposing view couldn't help but suffer by comparison. In fact, as he thought about it, he almost felt sorry for Dr. Zander. He was a good old guy, and he was going to look pretty foolish before this was over.

When the Monday program began, Matt started by introducing Dr. Zander, mentioning his credentials as a Bible scholar, and warmly welcoming him to the program. Then Matt read the Bible passage in question from Malachi 4:5-6: " 'See, I will send you the prophet Elijah before that great and dreadful day of the LORD comes. He will turn the hearts of the fathers to their children, and the hearts of the children to their fathers; or else I will come and strike the land with a curse.' That sounds pretty straightforward," Matt commented. "It says that Elijah will come before the Lord returns. Dr. Zander, I understand you don't think this passage can be taken literally for our time. Why is that?"

Zander, a rumpled-looking man in his sixties with an athletic physique and wildly uncontrolled sandy hair turning gray, responded, "When interpreting the Bible, we always need to compare Scripture with Scripture. In Matthew 17, we find an interesting application of this Malachi prophecy.

"Christ's disciples had asked him about Elijah returning, and Jesus replied, 'To be sure, Elijah comes and will restore all things. But I tell you, Elijah has already come, and they did not recognize him, but have done to him everything they wished.'

"We read in the next verse that 'the disciples understood that he was talking to them about John the Baptist.'

"Now, for me the words of Jesus are definitive. If Jesus said the Elijah prophecy was already fulfilled in his day in the ministry of his forerunner John the Baptist—and I believe he did say that—then the question is settled." He raised his eyebrows and smiled at Matt as if he had not only resolved the issue beyond all doubt but also had done so in the succinct manner Matt had called essential for a popular talk show.

"Well, perhaps not quite settled," said Matt, feeling the same almost triumphant buzz he had felt some years before when he'd nailed the World Trust Bank officers in their smug lies. "In John 1:21 we read that the priests and Levites asked John the Baptist, 'Then who are you? Are you Elijah?' and John replied, 'I am not.' "

"Now, Dr. Zander," continued Matt, "if John the Baptist was Elijah returned, I have to wonder why he flatly stated that he was not Elijah. Was he lying? Was he confused about his own identity?

"Quite frankly, it seems to me that John's denial is more clear and unmistakable than Jesus' assertion. The passage you read to us a moment ago says that the disciples *understood* Jesus was talking about John the Baptist. Maybe they understood wrongly. Jesus did not come right out and state it, as John came right out and denied it."

Dr. Zander smiled, seeming completely unmoved by what Matt thought a devastating question. "Interesting. But of course, even if I agreed that John the Baptist might not be the one Jesus had in mind, the fact remains that Jesus clearly said, 'Elijah has already come.' Therefore, we don't need to look for Elijah in our day, because Jesus said the prophecy was fulfilled long ago. I don't believe we have to look for Elijah or anyone else before Jesus returns. He could come any time. He could come today. Or he could come a hundred years from now. We just don't know.

"Nevertheless, I maintain that Jesus did refer to John the Baptist as Elijah. I think the apparent conflict between his statement and John's denial is resolved by a third Scripture—Luke 1:16-17—which describes John the Baptist as coming 'in the spirit and power of Elijah . . . to make ready a people prepared for the Lord.'

"Putting all these Scriptures together—as we must if we are to rightly interpret God's Word—we see that John was not literally Elijah, but he did come 'in the spirit and power of Elijah,' and he did fulfill the prophecy that Elijah would return.

"I might add," said Dr. Zander, "that this is not only my view. No, no"—his hair waved crazily with the vigorous movement of his head—"this has been the teaching of many other leading theologians down through the centuries, including Martin Luther and John Calvin."

* * *

On Tuesday, with Dr. Elaine Newman as his guest, Matt again set the stage by reading the Elijah prophecy. He then summed up Dr. Zander's argument that the prophecy was fulfilled in John the Baptist and no one therefore should expect Elijah to come again.

"I look at it quite differently," said Dr. Newman, a classy-looking woman, so well-dressed and immaculately groomed that Matt almost wished he was doing television instead of radio. "In reading the prophecy carefully, one sees that it does not primarily relate to the first coming of Christ, but to his Second Coming.

"Notice, it says that God will send Elijah 'before that great and dreadful day of the Lord comes.' The first coming of Christ was not the 'great and dreadful day of the Lord.' Jesus was born in Bethlehem in the humblest circumstances. He was cradled in a cattle stall, announced to lowly shepherds in the field, nurtured in the family of an obscure carpenter. He came as a helpless infant. His arrival had no immediate effect on the society of that time. That coming of our Lord simply was not a 'great and dreadful day.'

"By contrast, when Christ returns, it will be as King of kings and Lord of lords. His coming will be known worldwide and will dramatically change everything. The powers of evil will be overthrown and the Kingdom of God will reign on earth. This will be the 'great and dreadful day of the Lord': a great day for the righteous, who at last enter into their kingdom, and a dreadful day for the wicked, who finally face judgment.

"Now then, since the prophecy of Malachi clearly ties Elijah's return to the 'great and dreadful day of the Lord,' and since that is still future, it seems to me Elijah is yet to come."

"I must say that sounds very convincing!" said Matt. "But how would you answer Dr. Zander's claim that Jesus identified John the Baptist as the fulfillment of this Elijah prophecy?"

"Well, my interpretation does not conflict with the words of Jesus in any way. A great many Old Testament prophecies have dual fulfillment. For example, consider all of the prophecies about Christ coming as king. These were applied to his first coming, as when the wise men asked, 'Where is he that is born king of the Jews?' But we know that the only crown Jesus ever wore during his thirty-three years on this earth was a crown of thorns they pressed onto his brow when they crucified him. Jesus will literally reign as king only after his Second Coming.

"In the same way, John the Baptist was a partial or symbolic fulfillment of the Elijah prophecy. As the Scripture says, John came in the 'spirit and power' of Elijah. But that in no way argues against a coming literal return of Elijah.

"To sum up, I see no reason, on the basis of sound biblical exegesis, to discount the prophecy that Elijah will return."

"And would you say that could happen *here and now?*" Matt asked.

Dr. Newman flashed him an engaging smile to recognize his clever play on the title of his program. "It could," she said. "Or it could not. God is sovereign; it will happen if and when he ordains."

"All right!" said Matt. "Thank you, Dr. Elaine Newman. Friends, don't miss 'Hear and Now' the rest of this week as we continue our exciting series on 'Elijah—Shall We Expect Him?' Tomorrow we'll hear from John Profett, famous author of *1999*. He says other passages of Scripture show Elijah indeed will appear in these end times. We'll be taking your calls on the subject, too. I'm Matt Douglas. This is 'Hear and Now.' "

15

Matt and Profett had agreed that Tuesday evening would be a good time to meet. They would evaluate what the theologians had said and how they should proceed.

The meeting was set for the Douglas home. "I don't want you to fix dinner," Matt had told Priscilla when suggesting it. "You need to just rest and recuperate. I'll bring in some Chinese food. That way we can relax, and both of us can be there as John requested."

"That's sweet of you, honey," she said, "but I really don't mind fixing dinner. I'm okay, really I am. I'll be home all day anyhow, and I might as well fix a nice meal for us. John must get awfully tired of eating out or eating his own cooking all the time, don't you think?"

"I can't argue with you there," said Matt. "I know I sure would like a home-cooked meal if I were in his shoes."

Priscilla prepared a standing rib roast with little carrots and mashed potatoes. For dessert, she made the special cherry cheesecake that had always drawn such raves from her family. She actually enjoyed fixing the dinner; she seldom prepared anything so elaborate now that the kids were gone and she was teaching again.

Both Matt and Profett did justice to her dinner by commenting, between requests for second helpings, on how delectable it was. They were also in a jubilant mood over the Zander-Newman interviews.

"The programs were great," said Profett, "just great. I thought Dr. Newman came across as much more credible than Dr. Zander.

Of course, she should have, since she is right."

"She was convincing," agreed Matt. "It will be interesting to see how our audience responds over the next few days after they hear you and also have the opportunity to call in and discuss the issue.

"And then, for our next step, I have another idea."

"Great," said Profett, "let's hear it."

"I've arranged for the first 'Hear and Now' telephone survey," said Matt. "Listeners can vote yes or no on the following question: 'Will Elijah return before Christ comes to reign?' To vote *yes* listeners will dial one number; to vote *no* they will dial a different number. They won't talk at all; as soon as their call is answered, their vote will be automatically recorded and they can hang up.

"If we don't get a majority of *yes* votes, it will surprise me," said Matt. "But even a strong minority would be good when you realize that if we had asked the same question a week ago most listeners wouldn't have known what we were talking about.

"If this pilot program goes right, we can go national with it next," said Matt.

"Superb!" said Profett. "But—"

"But what?" said Matt.

"But we have to be sure we are ready," said Profett. "Spiritually ready." He paused. "That's why I wanted to talk with both of you together."

"Okay," said Matt. "I really think we are spiritually ready now. We weren't last week, but God used that horror we went through to unite us. Priscilla is one hundred percent with us now, aren't you, dear?"

Priscilla nodded and started to say something, but Profett interrupted. "That's all well and good," he said, "but we need to go a little deeper."

Matt took Priscilla's hand. "Meaning what?" he asked.

"Think about it," said Profett. "Why did the Lord allow Priscilla to go through her ordeal last week?"

"Well, we don't know fully," said Matt. "It's hard to understand. We just have to trust God even when we can't see why he allows some things."

"True," said Profett, "but we also know that 'whom the Lord loves he chastens.' "

"What are you saying, that the Lord chastened Priscilla for opposing you?"

"No, not for opposing me, but for rebelling against God and the leadership of her husband when—"

"Now just a minute," Matt began, but Priscilla checked him.

"Let him finish," she said. "He may be right."

Profett held up his hand to stop any further exchange between them. "I don't think either of you understands what I'm saying. How could you? You are captives of this culture in which you live." He paused. "Let me try to explain. Do you remember Jezebel?"

"Vaguely," said Priscilla as Matt nodded decisively. "She was the wicked wife of King Ahab and a sworn enemy of Elij—of—" She hesitated and looked confused as the thought rushed upon her. "Of yours."

"That's right," said Profett. "Now, it's important that you get the picture. Ahab was King of Israel. Jezebel was a nobody in Israel except by virtue of her marriage to Ahab. Yet she called the shots. Some people think this Hillary you've got now is pushy, and they're certainly right. But Hillary is a meek and quiet spirit compared to Jezebel. That woman totally manipulated her weak-kneed husband, Ahab, and used his power to impose her wicked will on the people.

"I could have handled Ahab. He would have listened to me. I could have led the nation back to God if it hadn't been for Jezebel." Profett's eyes burned with anger. "But she got her just reward," he continued. "Do you remember what happened to Jezebel?"

"Generally," said Matt, as Priscilla slowly shook her head.

"It's not pretty," said Profett. "She was thrown from an upper window of her palace by two of her servants and trampled by horses. King Jehu ordered a proper burial for her, but when they went to recover her body . . . Perhaps I'd better just read it to you from 2 Kings, chapter nine." He opened his big worn black Bible and read: "But when they went out to bury her, they found nothing except her skull, her feet and her hands. They went back and told Jehu, who said, 'This is the word of the LORD that he spoke through his servant Elijah. . . . On the plot of ground at Jezreel dogs will devour Jezebel's flesh. Jezebel's body will be like refuse on the ground in the plot at Jezreel, so that no one will be able to say, "This is Jezebel." ' "

"How awful!" said Priscilla, shuddering and moving closer against Matt on the couch.

"Yes," said Profett. "But being devoured by dogs reminds me of what almost happened to you. God intervened and frightened away those dogs who kidnapped you, before they devoured you. That was a warning to you to beware of the spirit of Jezebel.

"Unfortunately, this whole society"—he waved his arms in a wide, sweeping arc—"is infected with the spirit of Jezebel, Christians included. Only you call it"—his voice dripped sarcasm—"the feminist movement."

"We're hardly feminists," said Matt. "In fact, most Christians we know oppose the feminist movement, especially radical feminism."

"You think you're not feminists!" said Profett, his voice raised and his tone agitated. "But your women work outside the home, Priscilla included.

"That's why your divorce rate is skyrocketing. Women meet men in the workplace; they work together and next thing you know they're involved sexually. Working women also get to feeling independent because they have their own income. It all causes the breakdown of the family!

"Meanwhile, your children are going to hell because their mothers are not home where they belong taking care of them."

Matt nodded. "I know there's validity to what you say, in many cases. But Priscilla never worked outside the home until our kids were in college, for Pete's sake."

Profett was not swayed. "Older women are supposed to be examples to the younger," he said. "Priscilla is contributing to the Jezebel spirit rather than standing against it. And she's been infected by it as well. Otherwise, she would never have opposed the call of God on her husband, as she did last week.

"I'm telling you, what happened to Priscilla was a warning!" Profett's eyes were bulging and his fists were clenched. But then he visibly relaxed a little and his tone changed. "But God can reverse all of that. He can make Priscilla an example of what a godly woman should be."

Priscilla, who had been looking like a scolded puppy, brightened a bit at hearing the new hopeful tone in Profett's voice.

"There's more to this than you're grasping yet," said Profett, "and it's vital that you understand me. God's call on me is to prepare people for the coming of Christ. A big part of that is to stand against and drive out this wicked spirit of Jezebel.

"Here, let me show you another Scripture. These are the words of Christ," he said, turning to Revelation 2:20. " 'Nevertheless, I have this against you: You tolerate that woman Jezebel, who calls herself a prophetess. By her teaching she misleads my servants into sexual immorality.'

"See, there it is, exactly what I was telling you about men and women working together and getting involved sexually. There could not be a better description of your so-called Christian feminists than we just read from Revelation," said Profett, "and Jesus says we are not to tolerate them!" Again he was nearly shouting, and again he changed his tone to plead with them. "Dear Matt, dear Priscilla, how can I call God's people out of their error if I myself tolerate a Jezebel in my ministry? Don't you see, that's what I meant about the need to go a little deeper than simply to have your support, Priscilla. We need you to renounce the spirit of Jezebel and all that goes with it."

"I never thought of it like that," said Priscilla, tears in her eyes. "Maybe I have been influenced by the spirit of the age, but with all my heart I really do want to be God's woman. What do I need to do?"

"That job outside the home is the first thing," said Profett. "That has to go. Once you have proved your obedience there, we can talk about the next step."

16

In the broadcast studios of KOCB radio, Matt Douglas took a deep breath, looked across the interview table at John Profett, and launched into the Wednesday edition of "Hear and Now."

"Thank you, Mr. Profett," he began, "for taking part in our special series, 'Elijah—Shall We Expect Him?' On Monday and Tuesday we heard from two theologians with opposing views on that question. As the noted author of *1999* and as a speaker on end-time themes, what is your opinion?"

Profett smiled, winked broadly at Matt, and said, "It's clear from the comments of your previous guests—and I did listen quite carefully both days—that respected Bible scholars can and do differ on the issue. Without going back over the points they made so ably, I would simply suggest that other Bible passages not mentioned by your previous guests strongly support the clear statement of Malachi that Elijah will return before the Second Coming of Christ."

"Well, now, that's interesting," said Matt. "Dr. Zander emphasized that we always need to compare Scripture with Scripture in seeking correct interpretations. Are you saying there are some relevant Scriptures we haven't yet considered?"

"Definitely," said Profett. "Revelation 11 describes a three-and-one-half-year period when Jerusalem will be trampled down by the Gentiles and two witnesses will speak for God here on the earth. Verse 6 says, 'These men have power to shut up the sky so that it will not rain during the time they are prophesying.'

"Anyone who knows his Bible will recognize in those words a description of Elijah. As James 5:17 says, 'He prayed earnestly that it would not rain, and it did not rain on the land for three and a half years.'

"Get the picture now. In Elijah and in the two witnesses of Revelation 11, you've got the same power—to withhold rain. And you've got the same length of time—three and a half years. Are we to believe that is all just coincidence? Even though Scripture specifically declares that Elijah will return? I find that incredible."

"Very interesting," said Matt. "You believe Elijah is one of the two witnesses described in Revelation 11. If that is so, who do you believe is the other one?"

"I believe it's Moses," said Profett. "Verse 6 says the two witnesses 'have power to turn the waters into blood and to strike the earth with every kind of plague.' Again, Bible students will recognize that this is what Moses did in leading the children of Israel out of Egypt."

"Yes," said Matt, "and wasn't the departure of Moses from this earth shrouded in mystery, like Elijah's departure?"

"That's true," said Profett. "The last chapter of Deuteronomy says that Moses died, but 'the Lord buried him,' and no one was ever able to locate his grave. So we don't know what special plans God may have had for Moses.

"We do know, according to Matthew 17, that when Jesus was here on earth, both Moses and Elijah appeared talking with him on the Mount of Transfiguration. Matthew doesn't say these were ghosts or visions or apparitions of some kind. He says Moses and Elijah appeared. Evidently these two Old Testament figures were present here on earth when Christ lived among us, and they will be present again around the time of his Second Coming."

"Well," said Matt, "from what you are saying, maybe we should have called our special series "Elijah *and Moses*—Shall We Expect *Them?*"

"Maybe so," said Profett. "But I must say, the evidence is much stronger that Elijah will come, whether or not Moses ultimately appears."

"What do you mean, 'ultimately'? Are you saying that Elijah will come *before* Moses does?"

"Yes, that seems clear from the passages we've been citing."

"I'm afraid I don't follow you," said Matt. "Where does it say Elijah will come first?"

"Comparing Malachi 4:6 with Revelation 11 almost forces one to that conclusion," said Profett. "Malachi says Elijah will come *before* the great and dreadful day of the Lord to turn the people, *or else* God will strike the land with a curse. In Revelation 11 we see the dreadful day of the Lord arriving and the curse falling from the two witnesses, Elijah and Moses, on an unrepentant world.

"Clearly, Elijah has to be here preaching repentance for some period of time before the actual judgment, at which time Moses will be here too.

"This all makes perfect sense," continued Profett, talking much longer than Matt ordinarily let anyone go on uninterrupted. "Moses, as you know, represents the law and God's judgment. Elijah represents the prophets and God's call to repentance. Only when people refuse to heed Elijah and his prophetic call to repentance does God send Moses and his pronouncement of judgment.

"Today we are still in the prophetic era, the time of Elijah. God is calling people everywhere to repentance. But God will not wait forever. The great and dreadful day of the Lord is fast approaching. Personally I wouldn't want to move one day, not one hour, closer to 1999 without making sure I've repented and am ready."

Matt, at last realizing he had let Profett practically take over the program, spoke apologetically to the radio audience. "I'm sorry," he said, "if we seem to have gotten a little carried away here. This is a talk show, and not a sermon or Bible study. It's my fault, certainly, and not Mr. Profett's, and I do apologize." He paused. "All right, now, we'll be back after a brief message to take your calls on the subject 'Elijah—Shall We Expect Him?' This is 'Hear and Now.' I'm Matt Douglas."

Matt was hardly prepared for what happened next. Bob, the producer, stuck his head into the studio and said, "You guys must have struck a nerve. The calls are coming in hot and heavy. I hope you're ready."

When Matt got the signal that he was back on the air, he looked at the computer screen and said, "Hello, Judy from West Slope; you're on 'Hear and Now.' "

"Hello, Matt, Mr. Profett. I couldn't agree more with what you've been saying today. And Mr. Profett did *not* go on too long. In fact, if there's one message the church as well as the world needs today, it's the message of repentance. All we hear these days is 'love everybody,' and 'don't be judgmental,' and 'don't be legalistic,' which usually means don't have any standards. I didn't realize until now that the Bible foretells the return of Elijah, but I can sure see how we need him."

Chuck from Gresham was next, and he seconded everything Judy had said. "If America doesn't repent, God will certainly judge us," added Chuck, "or else he will have to apologize to Sodom and Gomorrah. God fried them for their sins—mostly perversion and homosexuality—and here in our country now, we are acting as if gays and lesbians are poor mistreated minorities. We've practically made heroes and martyrs out of them."

"You're exactly right, Chuck," said Profett. "Some churches actually ordain homosexuals, which is an abomination to Almighty God. But even our better churches have been caught up in the permissive spirit of this age. Christian women abandon their homes and families for the workplace, and practically no voice is raised against it. And when someone does speak up, he's told to be practical and face today's realities. Well, I'll tell you, Chuck, nobody ever said repentance was supposed to be practical in the eyes of this world. God is calling us to obedience, not practicality."

So it went all afternoon. Derrick from Vancouver was the first of only two callers to deviate from the line that Profett's summons to repentance was urgently needed and long overdue. Bob put Derrick through quickly in an effort to provide some balance.

"Everyone is cheering Mr. Profett's call to repentance," said Derrick. "But as usual they want someone else to do the repenting—like gays. I'd like to speak to your question, which seems to have been forgotten: should we expect Elijah?

"I'd answer that question with a no, because if that were true, it would mean Christ couldn't return today, for example, because Elijah hasn't appeared yet. I believe Christ could return at any time. I believe we should always be ready, not wait until some Elijah shows up and then repent in an effort to get ready."

Profett pounced on Derrick's comments like a cat on a mouse. "You don't disagree with me as much as you simply misunderstand my position," he said. "I believe Christ can return at any time too. He could have come back at any time since he left, almost two thousand years ago. God is sovereign and he can do whatever he chooses. However, Christ not only *can* come back but he certainly *will* come back when prophetic events reach a certain point.

"Now, some people believe Christ's return will occur in two stages: first he comes for his own, an event called the rapture, which could occur anytime; and then he comes with his own to set up his earthly reign. I'm saying Elijah will come before Christ returns *to reign*. So whether Christ's return is in one stage or two, the appearance of Elijah would mean the reign of Christ is soon to follow."

Frank from Tigard was next. He called Profett a "voice in the wilderness," and said, "What a refreshing thing it is to hear a preacher of prophecy be practical. Everybody wants to debate theories, but this man is telling us what we need to *do* about prophecy.

"Where *is* the preaching on sin and judgment and hell today in our churches?" Frank continued. "It has practically disappeared, and why? It's still in the Bible. I don't know whether Elijah is actually coming back or not, but I for one will do all I can to further the ministry of John Profett as the closest thing to it we have in the world today."

Before concluding the program, Matt mentioned the telephone survey he had arranged. "Tomorrow you will have the opportunity to register your opinion on the question of Elijah's return," he said, "simply by dialing a number. Until then, this is 'Hear and Now,' and I'm Matt Douglas."

✳   ✳   ✳

That evening, over dinner at the Douglas home, Matt and Profett reviewed the day. Since the two men needed to plan strategy, and thought Priscilla had little to do anyway but cook and clean, they had decided to eat their evening meals together at the Douglas home for a while.

"It couldn't have gone better," said Profett between mouthfuls of barbecued chicken and scalloped potatoes.

Matt agreed. "When we run the telephone survey tomorrow," he said, "I think we should word the question a little differently than I first planned. Instead of asking, 'Will Elijah return before Christ comes to reign?' let's ask, 'Will *an* Elijah return before Christ comes to reign?' "

Profett looked uncertain. "What's your thinking?" he asked. "Why would that be better?"

"It's easier to vote yes on," said Matt. "Judging by our calls today, I think the yes votes will knock the socks off the no votes if we word our question that way."

Profett still seemed uncertain. "Maybe we'd get more yes votes, but it's on a weaker statement."

"I'm thinking about momentum," said Matt. "Today's callers gave you a big boost. An overwhelming yes vote on the heels of those calls could put you right into orbit. 'Elijah' or 'an Elijah,' it won't matter much once you really take off. But the phrasing could matter a lot in terms of which way people vote tomorrow."

"I don't see it," said Profett. "I'm not *an* Elijah; I *am* Elijah. I think we can leave the question just as it is and still poll a majority of yes votes. That's what you said too when you first suggested the idea."

"That may be," said Matt, "but I just don't think it's our best strategy. Why write off all the people who can't quite yet sign on to a literal return of the literal Elijah? If we state the question a bit more broadly, we open the door to support from both those who can and those who for some reason cannot call you Elijah. Isn't it the message—'repent for Christ is coming soon'—that's important here, rather than your identity?"

"Both are important," said Profett. "My message and my personal identity stand or fall together. Here, look at the record." He picked up his Bible, which seemed to fall open to 1 Kings 18. "What does the last half of verse 36 say?" Profett asked, pointing to the text.

Matt read, " 'Let it be known today that you are God in Israel and that I am your servant and have done all these things at your command.' "

"See?" said Profett. "People have to know that I am God's servant and that what I do and say are at his command. I'm going to overrule you this time, Matt. But don't worry. God has given me assurance that we'll still get a strong yes vote."

Matt was silent for a moment. "Well, I guess I can't argue," he said. "The last time God gave you an assurance, it was about Priscilla's safe return. And we know how that came out." Matt turned to Priscilla, who had sat silently listening as the men talked. "Don't we, dear?" he said.

"You'll get no argument from me," said Priscilla, and she rose to clear off the dinner dishes. The men talked a while longer and then Profett left.

Less than an hour later Profett walked into an electronics superstore. He marched directly to the counter and spoke to the man working there. "Is my order ready?" he asked. "You promised to have it here by tonight." He pulled his copy of an order form from his billfold, along with a large amount of cash, and presented it to the clerk.

"Oh, yes, the automated phone dialing machine," the clerk said. He lifted a carton from under the counter and gave it to Profett. "Here you are," he said, "and thank you for your business, Mr. Douglas."

17

"Aiiiieeee!" Priscilla screamed.

Matt was jolted awake and sat upright in bed. For the third time since the rape, Priscilla was falling prey to a screaming terror in the night. Neither she nor Matt knew what to do about it, or even what it was. Her first day back home, she'd had a nightmare, reliving the rape. That was bad but at least they understood it. Since then there had been no nightmare, no dream, no flashback, just these night terrors.

He took her in his arms now, and noticed she was trembling, like each time before.

"How long will this go on?" Priscilla asked, a desperate quality in her voice.

That's what I'd like to know, Matt thought. *This is really getting old.*

"I lie awake half the night, and then I feel like a zombie the whole next day," Priscilla lamented.

Why can't she get hold of herself? Matt thought, but he simply said, "I know, it's tough."

"Maybe I did the wrong thing by not going after those animals," said Priscilla. "That's probably why I feel so down and defeated. They got away with it, Matt. They got away with raping me!" She began to cry with anger and frustration. "I wish they were *dead!*"

Matt's first thoughts were "love your enemies," and "vengeance is mine, saith the Lord," but he decided now was not the time to dump a sermon on Priscilla. As patiently as he could he replied, "Maybe we should have, but it doesn't do any good to second-guess the past. You made the decision you thought best at the time."

Priscilla drew away from his embrace, lay down again, and began recounting her experience at the hospital for what Matt figured must have been at least the tenth time. "The volunteer from the women's crisis center wanted me to press charges. I know she did. She said it was totally my choice, but she really wanted me to press charges.

"That would have meant I'd have been examined right away by doctors looking for evidence. I'd have been questioned by police officers—males. If they ever did catch the creeps, I'd have to identify them and then testify to every detail in court."

She paused. "The volunteer said that if I pressed charges, the women's crisis center would support me every step of the way. I should have done it, Matt. I should have done it."

Matt sighed wearily. "But you didn't, and your choice made a lot of sense. You wanted to end that nightmare, to put it behind you and get on with your life, rather than drag things on for months or years."

"Put it behind me!" Priscilla shook her head. "Wouldn't that be nice? I didn't know I would have to keep battling this thing whether I pursued charges or not."

"You don't *have* to," said Matt. "Let it go."

She glared at him. "Oh, just let it go, huh? That's all there is to it. I'm holding on to it and I just need to let it go."

"With the Lord's help, yes. Come on, Priscilla, you can handle this. You're my unsinkable 'Scilla Brown. And if you need human help, I'm sure that's available, too."

Following through on that thought he announced in his best take-charge manner, "Tomorrow we are going to find out what services there are for women who *don't* pursue rape charges. There must be support groups or something."

That said, he turned off the lamp beside their bed and settled down to go back to sleep.

"There is a support group," said Priscilla, her voice sounding small and weary. "I already know that, but I don't know if I should join it or not."

"Why not?" said Matt.

"I don't know whether it would help," said Priscilla. "And my schedule is so up in the air right now. I don't want to join a group and then have to drop out right away—if I go back to work."

Matt switched the light on again and looked at her searchingly. "I thought that was all decided," he said. "You're not going back to work."

"But it might help me return to normal," said Priscilla. "It would give me something to do besides sit around and relive what happened over and over."

Matt shook his head. "John made it pretty clear that we can't work with him unless we get rid of anything that smacks of a working woman or Jezebel spirit. I thought you agreed with that."

"I don't know what I agree with any more," snapped Priscilla. "I don't see why it matters what I think, if I'm just supposed to follow you blindly.

"I'm sorry," she said, almost in the same breath. "Honestly, Matt, how can you stand me?"

Matt turned out the light again and relaxed. "You've been through a lot lately," he said. "It's no wonder you're having a struggle. But I know you'll be just fine."

Matt turned over on his side and soon fell asleep.

Priscilla turned on her side as well and closed her eyes, but sleep wouldn't come. *When Matt touches me now, does he think of them and what they did to me? Does he still see me as the pure and chaste wife I used to be? Will he ever see me that way again?*

He's trying to act as if nothing happened, trying to make things just like they were before. But the distance . . . will life ever be right again for us? I hope so, but you can't unscramble eggs.

She wanted to give way to her grief. She wanted to sob out all the doubt and pain and guilt and sadness. But Matt was sleeping now. She had already disturbed his sleep once, and he needed his rest. He had things to do tomorrow—big things for God and John Profett.

In the darkness and loneliness of the night, she held back the sobs, but she couldn't stop the tears that squeezed past her tight-closed eyelids and wet the pillow under her cheek.

*   *   *

Matt got up at his usual hour the next morning. He ate his usual oatmeal breakfast and left for work at the usual time. Routine. Some would call it boring. Not Matt. His well-ordered life had never been boring to him, and now that the usual was coming to an end, he was almost mourning it.

And the routine was ending. This was the day he would submit his resignation to KOCB general manager Pete Andrews.

Besides feeling sad, Matt sensed an uneasiness chewing at his gut. He could ignore it. He could pretend it wasn't there and forge ahead. But that was how people got in trouble. And that was not Matt Douglas's style. No, he had to analyze this uneasiness, and somehow come to terms with it.

As he drove to the KOCB studios, Matt sorted through the possibilities. Were his instincts warning him of some danger he hadn't considered? Or was he just having the typical second thoughts of a person facing a major change?

As he accelerated to make a green light that had turned yellow, Matt speculated aloud. "Probably I'm suffering the shock of too many changes coming too quickly." A change of jobs would be stressful in and of itself. Add to that the incredible significance of his new role as John Profett's associate, and the trauma his family had just endured, and Priscilla's still-troubled state. No wonder he was feeling uneasy.

Priscilla's condition—that was another thing; he had a disquieting feeling that changing jobs now was somehow being disloyal to her. Logically, he couldn't see it. Whether he worked for KOCB or for John Profett, he had to honor both his job responsibilities and his family responsibilities. Which job he held should make no difference. Maybe this unaccountable feeling of disloyalty was just another roadblock Satan was putting in his path to keep him from fulfilling the call of God on his life.

Matt was still wrestling with his thoughts when he reached his office and scanned his incoming mail. One letter caught his attention. It was a plain white business-size envelope with no return address and a Portland postmark. To the left of his name and address, he saw the words PERSONAL AND CONFIDENTIAL.

Probably a crank letter, thought Matt, and he put it aside. He sorted through the rest of his mail and memos until he spotted what he was looking for. "Telephone Survey Results," it said across the top of the paper. Quickly he scanned the page. His eyebrows raised and a smile spread across his face. "Not bad," he said aloud. "Not bad at all." The question "Will Elijah return before Christ comes to reign?" had brought in a total of 6,278 calls. Of these 4,218 had said yes and 2,060 had said no, making the percentages 67.2 yes and 32.8 no.

With a great feeling of satisfaction, Matt put aside the survey and turned back to the rest of his mail. He picked up the letter marked PERSONAL AND CONFIDENTIAL, tore it open, and glanced at the salutation: "Dear Matt Douglas." Nothing significant there.

Following the salutation was a full page of type, and then a second full page, and then most of a third page. At the end, the letter was signed: "Someone Who Cares."

Hmmmph! More likely "Someone Who Has an Axe to Grind" or "Someone Who Wants to Set You Straight," Matt thought. Quickly, he began reading the first page. He saw no hint of criticism or confrontation. Instead, the writer was strongly supportive.

I want to thank you for your recent programs concerning the return of the Prophet Elijah. Thanks especially for today's program with John Profett, and for his much-needed call to repentance. I was pleased that your callers were mostly supportive, but strong opposition will surely arise.

God has given me a word for you. Thus saith the Lord to Matt Douglas: "Have I not commanded you? Be strong and courageous. Do not be terrified; do not be discouraged, for the LORD your God will be with you wherever you go" (Joshua 1:9).

Opposition from critics will be only one small part of the attack Satan will launch against you. His greatest assault will be directed against your personal life. He will try to discourage you. He will try to divert you from God's call by raising other concerns. He will attack you at your weak points. He will attack you where you think you are strong. He will tempt you to self-pity whenever things go badly. He will tempt you to pride whenever they go well.

I tremble for you. The great talents God has given you and the open door he has set before you make you Satan's target. But if you will "be strong and courageous" according to the word of the Lord, he will greatly glorify himself through you.

Many more paragraphs of exhortation, encouragement and Bible quotations followed, and Matt soaked up every word. It seemed just what he needed.

Still, doubts nagged him. He took his letter of resignation from his briefcase, fingered it for a few moments, then decided that before he took it to Pete Andrews's desk he would talk to John Profett one more time. He needed to call him anyway and tell him about the great survey results.

When Profett answered his telephone, Matt said, "Great news! We knocked 'em dead."

"What?" said Profett.

"The survey," said Matt. "It wasn't even close. We got over 67 percent of the vote, more than a two-to-one edge, 4,218 votes out of a total of 6,278."

"Good," said Profett. "Sounds like we're right on track. So you'll soon be announcing both the survey results and your resignation to become director of John Profett Ministries, right?"

"Yes, that's what we planned," agreed Matt, "but I—I—"

"You're not wavering, are you?" Profett said. "Matt, a double-minded man is unstable in all his ways. I thought better of you than that."

"I know," said Matt. "It's just that—well, you know what we've been through—what Priscilla especially has been through. She's waking up in the middle of the night screaming."

Profett was incredulous. "And you think she wouldn't if you'd betray God's call on your life? That would somehow make her suddenly all better?"

"No," said Matt, "I realize—"

"Can't you see what's happening here?" Profett said. "First it was Priscilla's opposition. Now it's her condition. Satan is obviously trying to use Priscilla to keep you from obeying God's will. That's the way Satan has worked from the beginning, Matt. Who did Satan use to tempt Adam? It was the woman, Eve. Who did Satan use to ruin Ahab? It was his wife, Jezebel. It's just so obvious, Matt. I can't believe you don't see it."

"I do see it," said Matt. "I didn't say I've changed my mind. I just had to work through some of these things. Actually, I got a letter today that has already helped me gain perspective on the spiritual warfare we are facing.

"As for my future with John Profett Ministries, you'll be pleased to know my letter of resignation from KOCB is already written and I'm holding it in my hand right now. As soon as I hang up from talking with you, I'm going to deliver it personally."

"Good!" said Profett. "And, Matt, I didn't mean to come down on you hard just now. But, you're right. We are in spiritual warfare. And you know, every once in a while a soldier needs a slap in the face just to keep him thinking straight."

Matt hung up the phone, picked up his letter of resignation, stifled his doubts, and marched resolutely down the hall to the office of Pete Andrews.

18

With his resignation letter delivered to management, Matt went to work next on an announcement for broadcast on "Hear and Now." He wanted to say things just right, so he worked over the wording carefully. Finally, he read the version that satisfied him:

Today I have a special announcement that I make with great joy but also with sadness. I have tendered my resignation to the management of Oregon Christian Broadcasting, effective next Friday.

I leave KOCB not because of any dissatisfaction on my part but because of the unique opportunity I believe the Lord has set before me.

Those of you who are regular listeners to "Hear and Now" are familiar with the ministry of Mr. John Profett. Our recent program in which he called the Christian community to repentance in preparation for Christ's soon return, drew unparalleled response. Many of you recognized, as I did, that this call to repentance is a much-needed and authentic message from our Lord.

I have been invited to become director of John Profett Ministries, with special responsibility for what we have named "The Elijah Project"—to facilitate the spread of Mr. Profett's message around our nation and the world.

This is not a decision reached hastily or based only on the "Hear and Now" broadcasts of recent days. It is rather the result of long and prayerful consideration.

Though I will no longer be host of "Hear and Now," I am pleased to tell you that this is not goodbye. As a part of the Elijah Project, Mr. Profett and I expect to inaugurate a new nationwide program soon that will be carried right here on KOCB. We call it "Countdown." Mr. Profett and I will cohost the broadcast, and we'll be joined from day to day by guests from around the country who can help prepare the church for our Lord's return.

We ask for your prayers and support.

This is "Hear and Now." I'm Matt Douglas.

* * *

By the time Matt's two-week notice to KOCB had expired, "Countdown" was ready for broadcast locally and well on the way toward getting on the air nationwide. The promotional tease to be aired on each station said:

John Profett, author of the bestseller *1999,* is as controversial as his book on Christ's return. Yet, after hearing him, two out of three respondents in one survey voted support for his message. Why? Hear him yourself and find out on the new program, "Countdown."

In early "Countdown" broadcasts, Profett pulled no punches. Using everything he had learned by means of the KOCB broadcasts, he indirectly claimed the mantle of Elijah and issued a strident call to repentance. He castigated gays, prochoice advocates, political liberals, radical environmentalists and all who sympathized with them.

While voicing those sentiments did not distinguish Profett from many other leaders, one message did uniquely characterize him. He denounced feminism and inveighed against its many subtle incursions into the Christian community. As he had with Priscilla and Matt personally, he now insisted publicly that even those generally opposed to feminism were deeply infected by it.

Meanwhile, in the Portland area, excitement over Profett and the claims being made about him rocked the city.

"Look!" said Matt, at a strategy meeting one day in his home office, now his principal place of business. He showed Profett a list of churches. "Within the past two weeks every one of these churches has featured at least one sermon related to Christ's return, to *1999*, to repentance, or to the proper role of women."

Profett took the list and studied it carefully. "Baptist, Presbyterian, Assembly of God, Community, Lutheran, Evangelical, Catholic. That's quite a list," he said. "Oh, and here's a Methodist and a Church of God, several Christian, Episcopal. Great!"

"Now, they haven't all been favorable to us by any means," Matt cautioned. "But they *are* talking about the issues we have raised. That means we have set the agenda. We have framed the issues. It's really quite remarkable!

"Things are cooking beneath the surface, too," he continued. "Rumors have spread all over town that you are Elijah. As a result, I've got a reporter from *America Today* wanting an interview with you. I told him I would make the arrangements. How about right here, tomorrow morning at ten?"

"Fine," said Profett, obviously pleased. "And don't worry. I'm not about to tell him I'm Elijah. As we agreed, I'll tell him that my ministry is to call people to repentance because Christ is coming soon. I'll tell him that's what I want to talk about and not about myself."

"Good," said Matt. "Now, there's one more thing we need to discuss. You know, I invited Dr. Elaine Newman to be our guest on 'Countdown.' She made such a good case for Elijah's return when she appeared on 'Hear and Now.' Well, she declined, and I thought she seemed rather cool over the phone. Now I think I may understand why. She's today's guest on 'Liveline,' the afternoon talk show on KPDQ, and from what I hear, she's, shall we say, a bit miffed."

"Oh?" said Profett. "What's eating her?"

"That's what I asked Lew Davies—he's been hosting 'Liveline' just about forever. Lew says she's concerned because the word is around that she has endorsed you when she actually hasn't."

"Do you think this means trouble for us?" asked Profett.

"I don't know; it could. Depends on what she says and how she says it. I thought maybe you'd want to listen."

*   *   *

At his home in Colton that afternoon, Profett tuned his radio to KPDQ. He listened as Lew Davies introduced Dr. Elaine Newman and she graciously thanked him for having her on the air. If she was upset, it certainly didn't show in her manner or tone of voice.

Lew began, "There's a great deal of excitement in our community just now over the ministry of John Profett. Many are strongly applauding his call to repentance, and some are speculating that he may even be the prophet Elijah, sent by God precisely for the purpose of preparing us for Christ's return. Others say such ideas are wrong at best and possibly dangerous.

"Your thoughts on this issue are of special interest, Dr. Newman, because you are being 'claimed,' as it were, by people on both sides of the debate."

"Yes," Dr. Newman said, "I am aware of that. I especially appreciate the opportunity to come here today, Lew, so that I may clarify my position."

Listening in Colton, Profett rose from his chair and went to stand right beside the radio. Here it came, Newman's statement, and he didn't want to miss a word, an inflection, or a nuance.

"Now," said Lew Davies, "you do in fact argue for a literal return of Elijah before Christ's Second Coming. Is that true?"

"Yes, that's true."

Profett nodded with satisfaction.

"And how do you see John Profett's claims in relation to your expectations?"

"I see no connection," replied Dr. Newman firmly. "I have never stated or implied that Profett is Elijah. Personally," she continued in her restrained, professional manner, "I cannot believe that he is Elijah, given his views on women, which in my opinion border on paranoia."

"Witch!" spat Profett. He grabbed his phone and dialed the number of Ray Dickson, the private investigator he had used earlier to check out Matt. "This is Gordon Finch," said Profett when Dickson came on the line. "I've got another job for you. I want to know everything there is to know about a Dr. Elaine Newman, who teaches at Seminary of the West. I particularly want to know any dirty little secrets she may be hiding. Do you understand?"

Profett listened a moment and then continued. "Deliver the information to the same drop box you used previously. And I'll pay in cash delivered by courier, just as before."

He hung up the telephone. "Women!" he spat out between clenched teeth. "Miserable Jezebels!"

19

H ow come you quit your job, Mother?" Diane asked. "I mean, I suppose it's nice not having to go to work every day, but—I thought you really liked that job."

It was the day after Thanksgiving and Diane and David had spent the holiday at home. It hadn't been quite the happy occasion Diane had expected with Grandpa Brown far away in Eastern Europe and her mother seeming depressed. Now Diane was probing for some clues to her mother's state of mind.

"Your father doesn't want me to work any more," explained Priscilla as she cleared the dishes after their late breakfast of blueberry muffins and coffee. "And neither does Mr. Profett. He says that a part of preparing the church for the return of Christ is to get Christian women back in their homes where they belong."

Diane stopped short in her rearranging of the placemats on the table. Her first reaction was one of indignation. What right had Mr. Profett to interfere in the private lives of her parents? Lives that had been well ordered for a long time before he ever appeared on the scene. Deciding not to overreact, Diane smoothed out the last placemat and sat down. "Well, that's not *so* bad in your case, I guess, although it's a bit much to say all women should be staying home. I mean the guy has to realize he's not living in Old Testament times, or even the 1970s.

"But, hey"—she decided to look on the bright side—"you've been saying you have no time to do anything around the house. Now, you can get at that bathroom you've been wanting to redecorate."

"Yes," agreed Priscilla, "I guess I can." She said it with a noticeable lack of enthusiasm.

Once she gets going on it, maybe she will perk up, Diane thought. "I know," she said, "let's go down to the Paint Bucket and I'll help you pick out some new wallpaper. Then, we can stop at the Good Earth for one of their walnut and alfalfa sprout sandwiches for lunch. Or would you rather go to the Olive Garden for soup and salad?"

"I do like the *pasta e fagioli* soup at the Olive Garden," said Priscilla.

"Good," said Diane, "let's go there."

* * *

At the Paint Bucket, Diane and Priscilla looked at wallpaper samples until Diane was nearly cross-eyed. Priscilla kept saying, "No, no, no." Occasionally she interspersed an "Oh, that's awful."

Diane was ready to conclude that, in her mother's frame of mind, nothing would please her, when Priscilla suddenly said, "Wait, I like this one."

"Oh, I like it, too," said Diane. "Those subdued little figures look great and I love this border. Paint the woodwork a light tan or almond and it'll be gorgeous."

Priscilla thought about it a few more moments, then headed to the counter. *Mission accomplished,* thought Diane as her mother placed the wallpaper order.

A short time later they were enjoying soft breadsticks, soup and tossed salad. At least, Diane was enjoying hers; Priscilla mostly just picked at her salad.

Diane tried to draw her mother out about how she was coping. "Dad told me the story about you and your old boyfriend, and how he ended up going with your best friend," said Diane. "Dad said that's how he came to call you 'the unsinkable 'Scilla Brown,' because you were so strong."

Priscilla responded with only a thin half smile and a weak nod, so Diane probed a bit more. "How did you do it? I can imagine how awful

I'd feel if Larry and, say, Cheryl pulled something like that on me."

"I felt awful, too," said Priscilla.

"But Dad said you handled it just—just *so well*."

"That's all he knew," said Priscilla. "He wasn't there when I first found out about it. I cried all day."

"Really? So how come you led him to believe you just shrugged it off, Mother? He still seems to think that's what happened."

"That's what he wanted to believe," said Priscilla. "Anyway, what was I supposed to do? Cry and carry on about another guy when I was going with your father?"

"But—but you're the one who first said you were 'the unsinkable 'Scilla Brown,' aren't you?"

"Yes, and that's who I am." Priscilla's voice grew resolute. "That's what every Christian should be. 'I can do all things through Christ who strengthens me.' "

That was the end of that conversation, but it didn't satisfy Diane. *"Unsinkable" and "can do" is all fine,* she thought, *but everybody has limits.*

✳   ✳   ✳

Back at Matt's home office, John Profett waved the latest issue of *America Today* under Matt's nose. "Did you read this article about me?" he demanded. Matt nodded. "That woman is out to get me!" Profett continued. "Listen to this: 'Seminary of the West professor Elaine Newman, once claimed as a supporter by Profett, has recently spoken out against him. In an exclusive interview with *America Today,* she said, "My supporting him would be like the hen backing the fox. If this man is as mistaken about prophecy as he is about women, those following him do so at their peril." ' "

Profett folded the newspaper and slammed it down on Matt's desk. "She couldn't just keep her mouth shut, could she? She couldn't say, 'No comment.' No, she had to try her level best to discredit me!"

Matt, always cool under pressure, saw the situation as a small minus but no major catastrophe. Still he understood why Profett would react to what he viewed as a personal attack. He wanted to put in perspective the probable minor effects of the adverse quote, without antagonizing Profett further by disagreeing with him. "It's too bad," he said, "but the article was quite fair on balance. You conducted yourself beautifully in the interview, and your emphasis on repentance came through nicely."

Profett continued undeterred. "Follow me at their peril, do they? She'll find out where the peril lies!"

"I suppose it's only natural that she'd disagree with you," said Matt, still trying to make peace. "After all, she *is* a woman in a mostly male institution. She probably feels threatened by your antifeminism."

"Matt, you are so naive," said Profett. "Always give people the benefit of the doubt, don't you?

"What you seem to have forgotten," he continued with a hint of sarcasm, "is the spiritual warfare we're engaged in. Satan is worried, and he's bringing out the big guns against us.

"There's no telling where her influence will stop," Profett raved on. "She'll probably be on Sandy Snavely's 'Talk from the Heart' program on KPHP next, and you know how popular that show is with the very people we most want to reach."

Matt wanted to disagree, but he knew it was true. The demographics for Snavely's show indicated that the strongest audience was among women aged 25-45 with families, above-average intelligence, and political involvement.

"She'll leave no stone unturned to ruin me," Profett continued. "I wouldn't be surprised if she wormed her way onto the Metro Catholic Broadcasting station too—what is it, KBVM?"

Matt shook his head. "Now that," he said, "is really unlikely. They don't even do talk radio; it's a good music station."

"She's a tool of Satan, and we've got to stop her," Profett said flatly. "It's that simple."

"But Elaine Newman is a godly woman," Matt protested.

"Oh, is she now? Maybe she was. But one by one she bought into Satan's lies. Now she's a big professor teaching men and usurping authority over them. And I can guarantee you, her rebellion against

God doesn't end there."

"What do you mean?"

"I mean," replied Profett, "that Newman is a lesbian, and she's up there at the seminary seducing young women she's supposed to be training for God."

"No!" said Matt. "That can't be! How could you possibly know that, even if it were true?" As he thought about the implications of Profett's accusation, his incredulity turned to alarm. "You haven't told anybody else about this, have you?"

"Not yet," said Profett.

"And you can't, either," said Matt. "You can't toss around dynamite like that. She could sue for slander."

"Let her," said Profett, "but I really doubt she would want to face her accusers in court."

"You've got witnesses?"

"If it comes to that, yes, but I think when the seminary administration gets wind of what's been going on, we can bid farewell to *Ms.* Newman."

"I—I don't know what to say," said Matt. "I'm just shocked." He rubbed his forehead with his hand, pushed the hand through his thick dark hair, and massaged the back of his neck. "But if you've got witnesses—if she really has been doing these things—she needs to be removed from teaching, that's for sure."

"That's right," said Profett. "It's our duty to expose the woman. How could we live with ourselves if we didn't?" He paused. "Tell you what, Matt. You set up a meeting between us and the seminary president. I'll take care of the rest."

"Yes," said Matt, his face troubled. "Yes, I'll arrange for it as soon as possible."

Profett left the office, a thin smile playing upon his lips. Women were so stupid.

20

D r. Elaine Newman walked down the hall of the administration building at Seminary of the West. She turned in at the door marked Office of the President. "Good morning, Alice," she said to the middle-aged woman seated at the desk in the outer office. "Dr. Lindsey wanted to see me?"

"Good morning, Dr. Newman. Yes, he told me to show you right in." She led Newman to the door marked "Dr. Merrill Lindsey, President." She knocked, then opened the door. "Dr. Newman is here," she announced.

Dr. Lindsey, a big, ruggedly built man with an ungainly stance, rose from his oversized padded-leather swivel chair and went to the door to meet Newman. "Thank you for coming, Elaine," he said as he shook her hand. Before closing the door, he turned to his secretary, "Alice, see that we are not disturbed, will you please?"

Elaine, meanwhile, was warmly greeting the third person in the room. "Jim," she said, extending her hand, "how are you? How are Doris and the kids?"

"I'm fine, Elaine," said Dr. James Conlan, distinguished-looking dean of faculty at the seminary. "Doris and the kids are fine. I have to tell you, though, that I am very upset right now."

"Sounds serious," said Newman. Until that moment it hadn't occurred to her that her sudden summons to the president's office boded trouble. Even now, she was inclined to assume the best. She looked from one face to the other and back again. "You gentlemen wouldn't be pulling some trick, would you, calling me on the carpet like this?"

"Sit down, Elaine," said Dr. Lindsey, unsmiling as he indicated a chair for her. Conlan sat down as well, and Dr. Lindsey returned to the swivel chair behind his massive desk.

"Elaine," he said, "some serious charges have been brought against you—extremely serious charges."

Elaine Newman looked at Conlan, who silently nodded in agreement.

"The charges," Lindsey continued, "allege certain improprieties between you and some of our students."

Newman frowned. "What sort of improprieties?" she asked. "And who is making these charges?"

Lindsey stroked his chin briefly, then folded his hands on the desk in front of him. "The allegations, Elaine, are that you are a lesbian and that you have seduced students into lesbian behavior."

Newman felt the color drain from her face. Her jaw dropped and she sat stone silent.

"These are only allegations," continued Lindsey. "We want you to know that you still enjoy our complete confidence. You certainly have a right to face your accusers and to be considered innocent until proven guilty."

Inside of Elaine Newman a kaleidoscope of emotions vied for dominance. Sadness, fear, anger, outrage and wounded pride swept over her. She struggled to maintain her professional composure. "Who are these accusers?" she asked when she had recovered enough to speak. She looked Lindsey straight in the eye.

Dr. Lindsey bowed his head for a moment. "We are told," he replied when he looked up, "that Marlena York, who left school here about two years ago, is prepared to testify against you."

"You are *told?* By whom? Who is behind this? Who is trying to destroy me?"

"We have not spoken directly with Marlena York," explained Lindsey. "We have a complaint from a prominent Christian leader, who has provided us with a copy of Miss York's sworn statement."

"What prominent leader?" demanded Newman.

"I'm not sure that's relevant," said Lindsey. "It is Miss York's charges you must answer." He picked up a sealed white envelope. "This is a copy of her statement detailing the charges. We would like your written response as soon as you can prepare it.

"Meanwhile, lamentable as it is, I have no alternative but to place you on immediate suspension. I'm sure you understand that the seminary cannot allow you to continue teaching until this situation is resolved."

Lindsey got up from behind his desk and walked over to where Newman sat stunned. He knelt beside her chair and put the letter in her lap. Then he took her hand in both of his. "I feel terrible about this, Elaine. If there were any way to spare you this unspeakable indignity, I would. I hope you know that."

He released her hand and stood to his feet. "Of course, the seminary will continue your regular salary until this matter is resolved, and you will certainly be in our prayers."

Conlan had also risen from his chair and now stood by as Elaine rose slowly to her feet. Both men accompanied her to the office door. "Will you be all right, Elaine?" asked Conlan. "Can I get you anything or do anything for you?"

She shook her head and walked out.

A few minutes later, back in her own office as she was preparing to leave for home, Elaine heard a knock on her door. "Come in," she said, and the door opened to admit James Conlan.

"Jim!" she said, surprised.

"Elaine, I feel just awful about this whole thing," he said, "and so does Dr. Lindsey. As soon as you left the room, he turned to me and said, 'You know, Jim, sometimes I hate this job.' He had tears in his eyes, Elaine!"

"I know, and I understand what a spot both you and Dr. Lindsey are in. What I don't understand is—" her voice broke and she fought back tears—"why would Marlena York want to destroy me?" She took a tissue from her purse and dabbed at her eyes.

"You had no personal dealings with her at all?" asked Conlan.

"No! And that's what puzzles me. I heard that she got into trouble after she left the seminary, even that she worked as an exotic dancer for a while. But I never even saw the girl outside class—either while she was a student or afterward. Why would she tell these terrible lies about me, Jim? Why?"

"The trouble is," said Conlan, "you're left to prove a negative. It's tough to prove something did *not* happen."

"Tough? It can't be done. Jim, you and I both know these charges alone are enough to ruin me, even though they can't be proven."

Conlan grimaced and hung his head. He had no answer. Then he said, "I think you have a right to know, Elaine, even if Dr. Lindsey doesn't think so. This whole thing was engineered by John Profett; he's the one who brought that statement to us and demanded action."

Newman groaned. "Now things are starting to make sense!" she said. "Of course! It's exactly what that misogynist would do.

"Thank you, Jim. Thank you for telling me. At least now I know what—and whom—I am fighting. And believe me, I intend to make a fight of it."

✳   ✳   ✳

Late in the evening of the same day, in the office at his home, Matt Douglas wearily drew both palms down over his face until his fingertips could massage his closed eyes. He had hated the meeting he and Profett had held with the seminary administration. He couldn't help feeling dirty about the whole thing, necessary as it had been.

But it was that way with any job; some bad always came along with the good. In most respects, these past days had been the greatest in his life. Much of the time he had felt euphoric over the rapid development of the Elijah Project.

"Countdown" was airing over more stations each day, and listener response was growing dramatically. Requests for John Profett interviews and appearances came with increasing frequency. Perhaps best of all, he had a sense that Profett's fame was spreading rapidly by word of mouth, a method he knew to be better than any amount of publicity.

As exhilarating as all this was, it was also consuming him. There was no way he could continue to administer everything himself. At a minimum he needed two key people right away. First, someone would have to handle finances: receive gifts from supporters, pay production costs, buy air time, pay salaries and other expenses, keep financial records. Second, he needed an office manager to attend to all the details involved in running an active organization. As it was, answering telephone calls was a task in itself.

Of course, having employees also required a place for them to work. His home office would never suffice, even if he were willing to give up Priscilla's and his privacy, which he was not. That meant he would have to rent office space and acquire desks, chairs, filing cabinets.

On top of everything else, he had to plan and produce daily "Countdown" programs, create and guide overall strategy, and extinguish brushfires—like this Newman thing—before they burned out of control.

With it all, he hardly had a moment for himself or for Priscilla. He felt bad about that, especially since Priscilla had been through so much. But once he got things organized, life could return to normal for them.

Okay, so maybe it wouldn't. Maybe he was caught up in something bigger than himself, something bigger than Matt and Priscilla and Diane and David Douglas all put together.

Profett had shown him a Scripture the other day. Matt had mentioned, just in passing, that he felt like he was neglecting Priscilla, and Profett had made him read 1 Corinthians 7:29. "The time is short. From now on those who have wives should live as if they had none."

Certainly, as Profett had pointed out, if the time was short when the apostle Paul penned those words, it was much shorter now. In such circumstances a man's duty to God had to take precedence over everything else.

Anyhow, so far as his relationship to Priscilla was concerned, a woman was created to be a helpmeet for the man, not vice versa.

Priscilla understood that, or at least she should.

It was now almost eleven, and Priscilla had long since gone to bed. Matt had removed the telephone receiver from the hook so he could work without interruption. Now, finished for the day, he replaced it. Almost immediately, the phone rang.

What now? thought Matt. As he said hello, he forced a smile, operating on the long held theory that the voice sounds more friendly when the speaker is smiling.

"Dad," he heard Diane saying on the other end of the line. "At last! I've been trying for the better part of two days to get you. Is everything all right? The line's always busy."

"I know," said Matt; "it's been a zoo around here. But you won't have that problem much longer. I'm getting a separate office and phone for the ministry. So, what's up? Problem at school?"

"Things are fine at school," said Diane. "I think the problem's at home."

"What?" said Matt. "Everything's okay here. Ridiculously busy right now, but okay."

Diane answered slowly, as if measuring each word. "They don't seem okay to me, Dad. Particularly, Mother doesn't seem okay."

"Well, she's still recovering," said Matt. "A person doesn't get over something like that just over night."

"I know that, Dad, but is she recovering? Or is she deteriorating? Every time I see her, she seems worse."

"Oh, I don't think so," said Matt. "You probably catch her on bad days."

"When are her good days, Dad? Almost two weeks ago, we went out together and picked out some wallpaper so she could redecorate the main bathroom. A week ago, I went and picked it up at the store because she hadn't. Now, she still hasn't started on the project—says she's too tired. What does she do all day?"

Matt remained silent for a long moment, then sighed heavily. "I'm afraid you've caught me at a bad time too," he said wearily. "Frankly I'm just too exhausted to deal with this right now. Let me think about it in the morning when I'm fresh, okay?"

"Okay, Dad," said Diane. "Are you going to bed right now, then?"

"Right now," said Matt.

"Good," said Diane, "because I'm a little worried about you, too." She paused. "I love you, Dad."

"And I love you," said Matt. "Goodnight."

He hung up the phone, shut off the office light, and went into the bedroom. In the dim light, he could see Priscilla sleeping. As he slipped out of his clothes, he thought about spending some time praying for her, but he was just too tired. Praying would have to wait until morning too.

21

Mr. Profett, Mr. Profett, I'm Paul Linnman, KATU-TV." Matt had called a news conference after Elaine Newman had spilled her story to the press, and Linnman wanted to ask a question.

"Mr. Profett," said Linnman, "Dr. Elaine Newman says you are trying to destroy her because you hate women and she dared to oppose you. What is your response to that charge?"

"My response, Paul, is that Dr. Newman doesn't need me; she is destroying herself. She made this matter public, not I. You know, I get pretty tired of it when people ruin their lives—and others around them—by their own sinfulness and then try to blame others. I preach *repentance*. If people would repent of their sins, they wouldn't be destroyed."

"A follow-up if I may," persisted Linnman. "You have said on your radio program 'Countdown,' and I quote you, sir, 'The wife and mother who works outside the home is in rebellion against her master and needs to repent.' Doesn't that lend credibility to Dr. Newman's charge that you hate women and see them as mere servants to their husband masters?"

"Not at all," said Profett. "The Master I referred to is God, who created man and woman and designed their relationship. It's true that I see women and men as different and having different roles. You and I have different roles also, Paul, and I don't think we should try to usurp each other's place. That certainly doesn't mean I hate you and all television reporters." He paused, then smiled broadly. "I'll leave that to the politicians."

There were other questions and answers, but all that aired on the evening news was the quote about Newman destroying herself while blaming it on Profett and the crack about politicians.

✳   ✳   ✳

In Newberg, Diane Douglas watched the report and wondered. It had been two days since she had called her dad about her mother's worrisome behavior, and they hadn't communicated since. She decided to call home.

After the third ring a voice answered. "If you are calling regarding John Profett Ministries, please press 1 now. If you wish to speak with Matt Douglas, please press 2 now. If you are calling about personal matters, please stay on the line and someone will answer your call."

Diane waited awkwardly as the phone at the other end rang about a dozen times. "Mother," she said when Priscilla finally answered. "I thought nobody was home. How are you?"

"I'm fine," said Priscilla in a flat expressionless tone.

"I see Dad got his new office and telephone. How's that working out?"

"Fine, I guess," said Priscilla in the same monotone.

"How's the bathroom coming?" asked Diane. "Have you got the paper up?"

"Paper? Yes, there's paper. I'm quite sure."

"Mother! I'm not talking about toilet paper; I'm talking about—" Diane stopped short. "Mother, is Dad there?"

"No, he hasn't come home from work yet. I hardly see him any more, he's so busy. And how are you doing?"

"I'm fine," said Diane. "Mother, what's Dad's new number at the office? I think I'll give him a call."

"Let's see," said Priscilla, "it's—it's, why I don't think he told me. Wait, yes he did. It's 669—no it's 696—something."

"Don't you have it written down?"

"Oh, yes, I have it somewhere. I'll look."

"That's okay," Diane said, "I'll just call information." But Priscilla had already put down the phone, and Diane could only wait. Finally, when she was almost frantic wondering what was happening, her mother came back on the line.

"Hello," said Priscilla.

"Mother, what took you so long?"

"I'm sorry," said Priscilla.

"Did you find the number?"

"No, it seems to have disappeared, but we won't let that stop us. It will take more than that to stop us."

"That's okay, Mother. I'll call and get it from the voice mail. You take care of yourself, and I'll see you soon." She paused. "I love you, Mother. Goodbye."

Diane's stomach churned with fear. She immediately dug a pen and some paper from her purse, dialed her home phone again, and when the voice said to do so, she pressed 2. "To reach Matt Douglas," the voice continued, "please dial 696-9208."

Diane dialed the new number and prayed it wouldn't be busy. To her relief, it rang. "Now, let him be there," she prayed. On the second ring, she heard the beautiful sound of her father's voice, live.

"Dad!" said Diane, "I'm so glad I got you."

"Me too," said Matt. "I'm afraid you've got me at a particularly bad time, though. Mr. Profett just arrived and we're up against a really tight deadline on 'Countdown.' But I can take a minute, what's on your mind?"

"It's Mother," said Diane. "I just talked with her, and she—well, she's been really depressed, but now she's hardly rational, Dad. Something has to be done."

"Oh, you're imagining things, Diane. What did she say that was irrational?"

"I—she, she couldn't even tell me your new phone number, and when I asked her if she had the bathroom paper up she thought I was talking about toilet paper. And she—she—"

"Your mother never could remember new phone numbers," Matt interrupted, "and the toilet paper thing—" he chuckled—"that's pretty funny. Sounds like she's getting back her old sense of humor."

"Look, Dad," said Diane, "I think I know Mother well enough to know when she's joking and when something's wrong. And something's wrong!"

"All right," said Matt. "All right." He paused. "I hate to ask you this, but can you take off a few days and come stay with her? That way you could keep an eye on her and satisfy yourself that she's okay."

Diane inhaled sharply and was about to insist once more that her mother clearly was not okay when her father added, "Or that she isn't. Who knows, maybe your being here would give her just the boost she needs."

"Miss several days of school? I don't know, Dad. I suppose it would be possible, but it's certainly not a good time for me. Besides, I think Mother needs *you*, not *me*."

"There's no way I can stay home and play nursemaid," said Matt, "especially when I don't think there's that much of a problem. You think about it, and if you decide you can come home, get Larry to bring you, okay?"

"I guess," said Diane glumly.

"Good girl, and now I have to go. 'Bye."

*   *   *

Larry Forrester lifted Diane's suitcase into the trunk of his car, then opened the passenger door for her. He walked around to the driver's side, slipped in behind the steering wheel, and started the engine. "I'm really sorry to hear your mother's having such a hard time," he said. "How long do you think you'll have to stay?"

"I can't stay more than a couple of days," said Diane as Larry turned his Olds 442 east into the stream of traffic. "Not unless I want to withdraw from school for this term."

As they drove along, Diane was preoccupied and unusually quiet. "It's a good thing your parents have the Lord to help them through hard times like this," Larry ventured. "If my mother ever went through what your mother has, she would be a basket case."

The words were probably meant to encourage her, Diane thought, but they were more disturbing than helpful. *Larry's mother would be a basket case? Her mother wasn't much better off.*

"Of course, my father wouldn't let it bother him too much," continued Larry. "Not as long as he could still chase around and get plenty of beer."

Diane tried not to think it, but the parallel was too obvious to miss. Her wonderful Christian dad was behaving just like Larry said his father would. Not drinking beer and running around, of course, but pursuing his own interests and refusing to be inconvenienced by the needs of his wife.

It almost broke Diane's heart to admit it, but what else could she think? It was the truth.

Meanwhile, Larry was wondering why Diane was making his attempts at conversation a monologue. He stole a glance at her and was alarmed to see tears running down her cheeks.

Larry felt helpless. He was keenly aware that he didn't understand women very well. Who could? Not knowing what to say that wouldn't likely make matters worse, he just drove on in painful silence.

Miles and minutes passed before Diane finally broke the silence. "It's Profett," she said.

"Profett?"

"Profett is responsible for my dad acting like a jerk toward my mother."

"What in the world are you talking about?" Larry asked, surprised.

"Dad is so much under that man's spell and so wrapped up in promoting him that he can't even see Mother's needs, much less meet them."

Larry felt like he shouldn't be hearing this. Diane was revealing things that were private between Mr. and Mrs. Douglas. Even worse, she was bad-mouthing Mr. Profett, an anointed messenger from God.

Diane talked on. "You know, that woman from the seminary, Dr. Newman, says Profett's a woman-hater. Maybe she's right. Since he showed up, it's been all downhill for my mother."

"I don't see how you can blame Mr. Profett for what your mother and father do," said Larry. "He's probably not even aware of their situation."

"I bet!" said Diane sarcastically.

"He couldn't be to blame," insisted Larry. "The Bible says husbands are to love their wives as Christ loved the church. Even I know that. Profett is a man of God, and he certainly knows it. He wouldn't encourage your father to violate God's word. I know he wouldn't."

"Maybe you're right," said Diane, "but I seriously doubt it."

They drove along in silence again for a few moments when Diane suddenly got an idea. "If you are right about Mr. Profett, all we'd need to do is inform him of the situation and he'd be on our side."

"Yes, I bet he would," said Larry.

"You know," Diane continued, "Mr. Profett is probably at Dad's office now, working on their 'Countdown' program. We could go there and talk to him."

"Just barge in on them?" asked Larry dubiously.

"No, that wouldn't work," said Diane. "I would need to see Mr. Profett alone. It would be humiliating for Dad to have me come there and ask his boss to straighten him out."

"Maybe we could go there," said Larry, thinking aloud, "and wait until they get through. Then when Mr. Profett leaves, we could catch him and talk with him privately.

"Or," and now Larry's face brightened and his voice rose, "I could go talk with him. I could take you on home to be with your mother, then go to the office and wait until Mr. Profett comes out, and have a heart-to-heart talk with him. I know he'll listen to me; he likes me."

Diane smiled. "You're sweet, Larry," she said, "but there's no telling how long you'd have to wait. You'd be dead on your feet tomorrow."

"I don't care," said Larry. "I'll take all night if I have to. You're worth it. Besides, I have a couple of boring classes tomorrow that I usually sleep through."

Diane snuggled closer and laid her head on Larry's shoulder. How ironic; here was a guy with no Christian background or family example, but he certainly knew how to treat a woman. She had never loved him more than at this moment.

22

Larry sat in his car outside the Sheridan Office Complex. He was positioned where he could see Mr. Profett's car, but where he would not be noticed if Mr. Douglas should happen to come out with Mr. Profett. He was pretty sure he had solved all the logistical problems of this operation, but he mentally rehearsed them again.

He had to intercept Mr. Profett somehow, without Mr. Douglas knowing. If he just waited until Mr. Profett drove away and tried to stop him on the road, there could be trouble. Mr. Profett might not recognize him and might think him dangerous.

He could leave a note, but what if the two men came out together? Mr. Profett might read it aloud or show it to Mr. Douglas and the secret would be out.

His solution had been to write a note: "Urgent I talk with you alone and without Mr. Douglas knowing. Am waiting in my car, a dark green Olds 442. Will follow you away from the office." He signed the note, "Larry Forrester (friend of Diane Douglas)."

Larry sealed the note in an envelope and wrote on the outside in large bold letters: URGENT and CONFIDENTIAL. He placed the envelope conspicuously on the windshield of Mr. Profett's car.

It was almost midnight when Profett, alone, approached his car. He picked up the envelope, opened it and scanned the contents, then looked around until he spotted the green Olds. He waved, then got in his car and drove away. Larry followed. A few blocks away, Profett turned onto a side street, pulled to the curb and stopped.

Larry stopped behind him, got out, and walked to the driver's side of Profett's car.

Profett rolled down his window. "Hello, Larry," he said. "I'm glad to see you again."

"You remember me?" asked Larry. He wanted to spare Profett embarrassment in case he did not remember, so he quickly added, "I met you at the Douglas home the day after you rescued Mrs. Douglas."

"I remember you very well," said Profett. "Get in and we'll talk." He cocked his head toward the passenger door to indicate where Larry should sit.

Once Larry was seated, Profett said, "Now, son, what did you want to talk about?"

"Well," said Larry, "I thought you ought to know what's going on in the Douglas family."

Profett nodded, and Larry continued. "Diane is really worried about her mother. She thinks Mrs. Douglas may be having a nervous break-down. And she says Mr. Douglas isn't helping matters any." Larry kept slipping his car key off and on his key ring as he talked. "To be perfectly honest, sir, she partly blames you. She says—" he hesitated. "I mean *she* doesn't say it, but she has *heard* that you are a woman-hater."

"And she believes that?"

"Well," Larry grimaced, "let's say she wonders."

"And what about you, Larry? Do you believe I am a woman-hater?"

"No, I think that's ridiculous," said Larry. "But I told her I'd talk with you and let you know how serious things are."

"And what do you think I should do about the situation?"

"I don't know," said Larry. "I thought maybe you could talk to Mr. Douglas, remind him what the Bible says about a husband needing to love his wife as Christ loves the church. Maybe even tell him to take time off from work until he gets his home in order."

"Larry, you are a man who believes the Bible and wants to live by it, am I right?"

"That's right," said Larry.

"I'd like you to read a verse." Profett picked up his big worn Bible from the middle of the front seat, switched on the dome light, and quickly turned to Hebrews 12. "What does it say here?" he asked, pointing to verse 6.

Larry read, " 'Because the Lord disciplines those he loves, and he punishes everyone he accepts as a son.' "

"See?" said Profett.

Larry slowly shook his head. "I'm afraid not," he said.

" 'The Lord disciplines those he loves,' " said Profett, punching his finger at each word as he read it. "It goes on to say he 'punishes everyone he accepts as a son,' right?"

"Right," Larry said tentatively.

"Though it says 'son,' we are not such chauvinists as to think it excludes women, are we?"

"No, but I still don't see—"

"You said husbands are to love their wives, and I'm telling you that you're right about that, but sometimes to love people requires that we discipline them. In fact, this verse says God disciplines *everyone* he loves.

"Mrs. Douglas is under discipline, Larry. She has some problems, and God is helping her correct them. This is not something that Mr. Douglas should short-circuit if he loves her. Much less should you or I interfere."

"But Mrs. Douglas is falling to pieces, according to Diane. She's having a terrible time."

"Yes," agreed Profett, "and the Scripture covers that as well. What does this verse say right here in the same passage?"

Larry followed Profett's finger down to verse 11 and read, " 'No discipline seems pleasant at the time, but painful. Later on, however, it produces a harvest of righteousness and peace for those who have been trained by it.' "

"Now, please, Larry, don't misunderstand me. I'm not saying Mrs.

Douglas is a terrible woman. Actually, I'm sure she is a godly woman in most ways. But like most other women of this age, she has been profoundly influenced by feminism and does not maintain a proper godly submission to her husband. She has what is called the spirit of Jezebel. Do you understand what that means?"

"Yes, I do," said Larry. "I'm a regular 'Countdown' listener, and I think you've explained the spirit of Jezebel very well on your broadcasts."

"Do you also understand, Larry, how hard all of this is for Mr. Douglas? None of us likes to see someone we love suffer. Mr. Douglas needs our support, Larry, not our criticism."

"I never thought of it like that," said Larry.

"There's something else you may not have thought of," said Profett. "Diane has grown up drinking from the same broken cistern as her mother. It would be a miracle if she didn't have some Jezebel attitudes. I hope you realize how absolutely critical to your success as God's servant is the woman you choose as your partner. Adam, King David, King Solomon, King Ahab—so many of God's choice servants were brought down to the dust of defeat by their women.

"For some reason, when I think of you, Samson comes to my mind. He was such a mighty warrior for God, as I believe God intends you to be. But Samson was ruined by a woman. He ended up a blind slave of the Philistines because he didn't have the strength to stand uncompromising against the pleas and tears of Delilah. Promise me, Larry. Promise me you will not be the Samson of our generation."

"I promise," said Larry. "and thank you! Thank you for believing in me."

23

Larry drove home that night with the words of John Profett reverberating in his mind. "I think of you as a mighty warrior . . . a Samson of this generation . . . don't let a Delilah bring you down."

Larry didn't think Diane was a Delilah. On the other hand, as Profett had said, she was almost certainly infected with feminism to some degree.

One thing was sure; he couldn't take any chances with God's will for his life. He would have to test Diane. To the degree that she exhibited the spirit of Jezebel, he would help her overcome it. And if she rebelled—surely she wouldn't, but if she did—he would cooperate with God in her discipline.

The next morning, before his first class, Larry called Diane. "How did it go?" she asked eagerly. "Were you able to talk with Mr. Profett?"

"Sure did," said Larry. "He's easy to talk to. Didn't I tell you he likes me? He did give me a little different slant, though, on your dad and mom."

"Yeah?" said Diane skeptically. "What do you mean?"

Here goes, thought Larry, *I hope she's spiritual enough to accept this.* "Have you ever heard Mr. Profett speak about the spirit of Jezebel?" he asked.

"Is the Pope Catholic? Anybody who has heard 'Countdown' has heard Profett speak about that subject. He's obsessed with it. He talks about that more than he does about *1999*."

"But have you taken it to heart?"

"What is that supposed to mean?" Diane shot back. "Are you saying I have this so-called spirit of Jezebel?"

"No," said Larry. "I'm just saying it's easy to hear a message and even agree with it but not apply it to your own life."

"So?"

Diane wanted to tell him she *didn't* agree with it, that she was beginning to think this guy was nuts. But she didn't really want to start down that road yet with Larry. He was too much of a Profett fan.

"So, Mr. Profett says your mother has shown the spirit of Jezebel and therefore she is being disciplined."

"That is just about the stupidest thing I ever heard in my life!" said Diane. "My mother is no more a Jezebel than—than—than that phony is Elijah!"

"Watch it!" said Larry. "Don't say anything you'll regret. It's dangerous to speak against a servant of God."

"Oh, excuse me! Somehow I got the idea that my mother is a servant of God, too. How come Profett's free to say whatever stupid thing he wants to about her, but I can't say anything about him?

"Honestly, Larry! I can hardly believe this! You spend one hour with this guy and he turns you around 180 degrees! You go to ask Profett to show some consideration for my mother, and you come back spouting his garbage about 'disciplining' her. She's not a child, Larry. She doesn't need Profett's discipline. She's hurt, and she needs some love and care."

"You're upset," said Larry, in the most patronizing understatement Diane had yet heard. "Let's talk about this some more later. I'm sure you'll feel different after you've had a chance to think."

Diane boiled. How arrogant could a person be? Didn't Larry think there was even the slightest chance that *he* could be wrong? That *he* might see things differently after he thought about it?

She decided not to challenge him. "Okay, Larry," she said with a disgust she tried to keep out of her voice. "We'll talk later."

✳   ✳   ✳

Diane hadn't even talked with her mother yet. Priscilla had been in bed when Diane arrived the previous evening, and she had not yet risen this morning. Finally, about nine Diane heard a stirring in the hall and then she saw her mother coming into the kitchen.

Diane was shocked at her mother's appearance. Her hair was uncombed. She still wore her nightclothes, over which she had pulled a robe. She wore no makeup. Her face looked puffy and swollen, and, most noticeable of all, her once shining eyes had become dull and vacant.

Tears sprang to Diane's eyes. She didn't want to cry. She wanted to be strong and buoyant and encouraging to her mother, but she couldn't help herself.

"Oh, Mother!" Diane embraced her, burying her face in the tangled hair.

Priscilla just stood there, not seeming to notice that Diane was crying, not wondering why she was at home when she should have been at college, not even returning her embrace.

✳   ✳   ✳

Diane stayed all day with her mother, who spent most of her time sitting and staring. Diane thought about what she would say to her father when he came home. And to Larry when she saw him again. Some of her thoughts were hard; men could be so maddening. But she reminded herself that these were both good men; they just didn't understand. She had to make them understand.

In the early afternoon, the phone rang. Diane answered, because she had noticed that every time someone called, her mother just sat unmoving for a long time. If the caller didn't give up, Priscilla would finally drag herself from her chair to the phone as if that simple task required huge effort.

The caller this time was her father. "Sorry I didn't get to see you this morning," he said, "or last night for that matter. But I'm glad you're there. How is everything?"

"Not good," said Diane.

"What's the problem?"

"I've told you what the problem is, Dad! Mother needs help, probably professional help, and she needs you to pay a little attention and act like you care whether she lives or dies."

Diane regretted the cutting words as soon as she had spoken them. She had not intended to lash out like that. Just this morning she had recalled some Sunday-school memory verse about grievous words and had looked up the passage in Proverbs 15: "A gentle answer turns away wrath, but a harsh word stirs up anger."

Now she had spoken the harsh word.

Her father didn't say anything for the longest moment. "I'm disappointed in you, Diane," he said finally.

"I'm sorry I put it that way, Dad," she replied.

Matt continued as if he had not heard her. "Mr. Profett told me I had a problem, and I could hardly believe him. But once again I see he's right. I never expected this kind of disloyalty from you, Diane."

"Disloyalty?" echoed Diane.

"What would *you* call it?" her father asked. "You told Larry I was neglecting your mother. You had him sneak around behind my back and talk to Mr. Profett about me. You had him ask Mr. Profett to suspend me from my job. That was a shabby thing to do, Diane.

"And I'll tell you another thing. If ever I doubted what Mr. Profett says about the spirit of Jezebel, I can sure see it now. In you!"

Diane could hardly believe her ears. She had been willing to apologize for her harsh words, but her father was way beyond that. Profett had not only poisoned Larry's mind against her, but he had twisted everything to her father too.

"He *told* you about Larry's visit?" Diane asked indignantly. "Profett is supposed to be a man of God, and he can't even keep a confidence that any respectable professional would keep? The man is crazy, Dad. Or evil."

"I won't have you talking that way, Diane. You are messing with spiritual powers you don't understand. Satan is out to derail Mr. Profett's ministry any way he can. And he will use anybody he can. But it won't work. Do you understand me? *It won't work!"*

With that he slammed down the phone.

Diane, trembling, slowly hung up the receiver. Never in her life had her father spoken to her like this. She wanted to call him back, to tell him he was right and she was sorry, to sooth the hurt and take away the anger in his voice.

But she also needed to heal her own hurt. She felt abandoned and cut off. She had always enjoyed her father's approval, and she wanted it now. She not only wanted it but needed it—needed it so badly that without it she felt incomplete.

One thing kept her from dialing his number. She knew with a knowing beyond her own understanding that he was wrong—terribly, tragically, unquestionably wrong.

It was remarkable, as she thought about it, how sure she was. If these were ordinary circumstances and she needed guidance on some question, she would talk with her mother or father. Or she would confide in her roommate Suzie. Or she would talk with her Grandpa Brown or perhaps Pastor Davis, who had been at their church all during her growing-up years. But now, with all these options closed to her, God had given her a certainty no amount of advice could have equaled.

Her certainty, however, did nothing to relieve her growing fears. Her family was falling apart, and even Larry was turning against her. There was still David, untouched so far as she knew by the insanity, but he had never been a strong Christian. What would this do to him?

She saw her mother sitting and staring, a shadow of her former vibrant self. "Oh, God," prayed Diane silently, "my mother is not unsinkable, and neither am I. We are sinking right now. Please, help us!"

In her mind's eye, Diane saw a scene from the New Testament. The apostle Peter was sinking in the Sea of Galilee and crying out to Jesus for rescue. Jesus reached out his hand and lifted Peter up.

In an instant she saw and felt herself being lifted above the wind-blown waves of the storm that had engulfed her life. "Thank you, Lord," she said. "Thank you!"

*   *   *

Matt had scarcely hung up the phone on Diane when it rang again. He thought perhaps she was calling back to apologize, but when he answered, a man's voice said, "Hello, is this Mr. Douglas? Matt Douglas?"

"Yes, it is," said Matt. "How may I help you?"

"I'm glad I've finally reached you," said the voice. "This is Lanny Crandall from Allbest Electronix. There's been an urgent recall issued for the automated dialing machine you purchased. That particular model has a defect that poses a risk of electrical shock to the user. We'd like you to bring it in and exchange it for a replacement model. No charge, of course."

"There must be some mistake," said Matt. "I never bought any such machine."

"Are you sure?" asked the caller, obviously unconvinced. "According to our records, a Matt Douglas purchased one on special order on November 12. You are the only Matt Douglas we can locate in the Portland area."

"It's a mistake," said Matt, "but thanks for calling." He hung up and dismissed the incident.

24

That night Matt's sleep was disturbed by strange dreams, and he arrived at work still troubled about them.

"I need to talk with Mr. Profett just as soon as he gets in," Matt told Shelly Green, his new office manager. The former KOCB receptionist had proved a life saver. Since he had worked with her before, Matt hadn't needed to worry about unforeseen habits or quirks spoiling things.

He had hesitated at first to hire Shelly because he sensed that there had always been a certain chemistry between the two of them. Not that there had ever been even a hint of any impropriety—but something could happen.

In the end he decided he'd just have to see to it that nothing did happen, like he always had. After all, where else could he find a single woman so efficient? And Profett certainly wouldn't have some Jezebel married woman who belonged at home. Shelly was also willing to work overtime during these hectic early days.

Today, John Profett would be flying in from a two-day trip to Phoenix. He had appeared on "God's Way," the flagship program of the Gospel Broadcasting Network. Matt had arranged that appearance as well as a private meeting between Profett and Peter Seton, head of GBN. Matt had developed a pilot TV version of "Countdown," and the two men were to discuss the possibilities of airing it over the worldwide GBN network.

Though Matt was eager to hear how that discussion had gone, he even more urgently wanted to tell Profett about the troubling dream he'd had. Matt often dreamed, of course, like everyone else. Most dreams he quickly forgot or dismissed. This dream was different. Matt couldn't shake the feeling that it meant something. That was why he needed to tell it to somebody. Somebody not too close, since it was embarrassing.

Just before three, Shelly ushered Profett into Matt's office. He had come directly from Portland International Airport, and one look at him told Matt the news from Phoenix was good.

"I'm glad to see you're smiling," he told Profett. "Does this mean 'Countdown' will be on TV soon?"

"It's a done deal," Profett said, beaming. "All that remains is for you to work out a few details."

Matt and Shelly grinned at each other, and she flashed a big thumbs up.

"I don't mind telling you, Matt," continued Profett, "that you deserve a lot of credit. Seton was very favorably impressed with your proposal and the pilot program. He said it was as excellent and professional a job as he's seen.

"Congratulations, Matt!" He grasped Matt's hand and shook it vigorously.

"And thank you too, Shelly. I know you've put in a lot of extra hours getting the Elijah Project off the ground. I want you to know I deeply appreciate it."

"Thank you," said Shelly, smiling demurely. She turned to leave the room, as did Profett.

"Before you go," Matt said to Profett, "I need to talk with you. If you have a few minutes."

"Of course," said Profett. Shelly smiled, nodded, and left the room. "What's on your mind?" asked Profett when she had gone.

"I had a dream," said Matt. He hesitated nervously, then cracked, "and I'm not even black."

"What?" said Profett.

"You know," said Matt. "I have a dream? Martin Luther King Jr.? Oh, forget it! Just a feeble attempt on my part to be funny, and it wasn't."

"You had a dream?"

Matt nodded. "Now, please understand, I don't usually put much stock in dreams. And I'm not saying this is an exception, either. But it's bothering me, and—well, I thought maybe you could tell me what you think about it."

"Certainly," said Profett, sitting down and loosening his tie. "Go ahead."

"Well," said Matt, stalling, "it was pretty bizarre. I wouldn't want you to think that I'm anything like I appear in the dream."

"Look," said Profett impatiently, "if you'd rather not tell me—"

"No!" said Matt. "I want to tell you. I need to tell you, so that I can either forget the whole thing, or—or heed the warning, if you think there is one."

"Okay, go ahead then." Profett sat waiting, so Matt took a deep breath and plunged into his story.

"In my dream, my daughter Diane and another young woman—I don't know who she was—went, at my direction, to a remote highway junction over in the Eastern Oregon high desert country. There they posted themselves up over the middle of the intersection like traffic lights, or like Jesus on the cross. They were both completely naked.

"About that same time, I arrived at the intersection aboard a bus. Motorists were already stopping to stare, but the bus driver proceeded right on through the intersection. Just around the next curve, I got off the bus and walked back to our rendezvous at the intersection. I was carrying a rifle, which I didn't even understand how to use.

"Police cars were converging on the site by now, and there was an awful sense of imminent confrontation. It was me against a small army of police, with bystanders gawking and the two girls being used as pawns."

Matt heaved a huge sigh and paused, stealing a look at Profett to see how he was reacting. Profett seemed to be taking it all in stride, so Matt continued.

"Now, this next part sounds even more like it's right out of a B movie," said Matt, "but so help me, it's exactly what happened. I woke up and just at that moment a flash of lightning lit up the room and a thunderclap shook the house. After a few more thunderbolts, but not a drop of rain, the storm passed, and I went back to sleep.

"I dreamed again, and this time I was back at my alma mater, Multnomah School of the Bible. I had arranged a public meeting there to show a video about the Elijah Project, and a large crowd had gathered. We had only begun the presentation when authorities from the school came in and insisted we stop. Something about the video was objectionable to them—I don't know what. In any case, I was determined to continue.

"Defying the authorities, I announced that the video would be shown, and we proceeded. They left, and I thought we had prevailed, when suddenly the video stopped. They had simply shut off the electrical power to the room. I was completely and very easily stymied. I felt so stupid!"

Now he looked at Profett, studying his face for a reaction.

Profett sat perfectly still except for stroking his beard, and he simply said, "Hmmm."

"So what do you think it means," Matt ventured, "if anything?"

"Well," said Profett, "you've had a lot more time to think about it than I have. What do you think it means?"

"Well, for one thing," said Matt tentatively, "the two dreams seemed to me like one, like Pharaoh's dream that Joseph interpreted."

"Now, let's see," said Profett. "As I recall it, Pharaoh dreamed he saw seven fat cows devoured by seven lean cows. Then he dreamed again and saw seven full heads of grain devoured by seven thin heads of grain. Joseph told him both dreams meant that seven years of plenty would be followed by seven years of famine in Egypt. Right?"

"Right," said Matt.

"Well, I'd say offhand that Pharaoh's two dreams were much more alike than yours. I don't see much similarity between a pair of nude girl traffic signals and a canceled video showing."

"I agree that the circumstances in my two dreams were totally different," said Matt. "But that only underscores their basic similarity. Look past the details and the dreams are almost identical."

"How so?"

"Well, for one thing, there was my desperate behavior. In the first dream, it was at my instigation the girls were displayed nude. That would be a desperate act in itself. And a despicable one; I would never exploit Diane like that! Or any other woman! Then, I was carrying a rifle, which I was untrained to use, against a whole cadre of armed policemen. How desperate can a person get?

"In the second dream, I was desperate enough to openly and publicly defy Multnomah authorities, which is pretty much out of character for me.

"I was also very stupid in both dreams. My schemes had no chance of working. I mean, for the Multnomah people to turn off the power was an obvious tactic, and yet it caught me by surprise and totally thwarted my plans. And the rifle thing was even more stupid, given the likely consequences.

"Also, both dreams involved highly public settings, and both pitted me against authority figures, which, again, is out of character for me."

"I see what you're saying," said Profett, "and you very well may be right. Beneath the surface, the dreams are extraordinarily similar."

"What troubles me most," said Matt, "is this." He picked up the Bible from his desk and opened it where he had placed the ribbon marker in Genesis 41. In a voice strained with emotion, he read verse 32: " 'The reason the dream was given to Pharaoh in two forms is that the matter has been firmly decided by God, and God will do it soon.' "

He looked at Profett, almost pleading with his eyes. "Is God telling me I am going to stupidly self-destruct, and it's certain, and soon?"

"Hmmm, I don't know what it all means," said Profett. "Perhaps nothing. Or perhaps you have misinterpreted it. At least, partly."

"Partly?" echoed Matt. "What part? What do you mean?"

"The stupidly self-destructing part," said Profett. "Just because you felt stupid doesn't mean you were."

"I don't follow you at all," said Matt.

"Look," said Profett. "All I can do is tell you what God has shown me about my own future. It's not that much different from your dreams."

"I still don't understand. You have had similar dreams?"

"No, I haven't. But I do read my Bible. Remember when I told you and your 'Hear and Now' listeners that Elijah is one of the 'two witnesses' foretold in Revelation?"

"Yes," said Matt uncertainly, "but I don't see—"

"Revelation tells me what the end of my story is going to be. I don't need any dream to tell me. Here, let me see your Bible a minute."

Matt handed over his Bible, and Profett turned to Revelation 11:7 and began reading: " 'Now when they have finished their testimony, the beast that comes up from the Abyss will attack them, and overpower and kill them. Their bodies will lie in the street of the great city, which is figuratively called Sodom and Egypt, where also their Lord was crucified. For three and a half days men from every people, tribe, language and nation will gaze on their bodies and refuse them burial. The inhabitants of the earth will gloat over them and will celebrate by sending each other gifts, because these two prophets had tormented those who live on earth.'

"I am going to die a violent death," said Profett. "I know that. This godless generation may listen to me now for a while, but sooner or later I'm going to be killed. And, like in your dream, become a spectacle in the street. I notice, too, that it will be the authorities who pull the plug on me. I mean on *me* literally, not just on my video."

He paused. "Don't look so shocked, Matt. Everybody has to die sometime. Wouldn't you rather go out with God in a blaze of glory than sell out to the devil and die a coward, a traitor? I know I would."

Profett rose from his chair, walked over to Matt, and patted him on the shoulder. "Don't worry," he said. "You'll get used to the idea." Then he walked out.

25

Profett's evening of reading at home was disturbed by the telephone ringing.

"Hello," he responded.

"Hello," said a strangely familiar voice. "Is this John Profett?"

"Yes, it is," said Profett. "How may I help you?"

"I heard you on 'Countdown' today," said the voice. "I've also read your book, *1999*."

"Yes?" said Profett.

"Both were very impressive. I'm glad to see you doing so well."

"Who is this?" asked Profett.

"This is your old friend Dick Thomas."

"Dick Thomas? I'm sorry; I don't know any Dick Thomas."

"Of course you do, Marcel," said the voice. "Don't you remember? Missoula Bible College, 1974. Your roommate."

For a moment Profett just held the phone in shocked silence as his mind raced to assess the implications of what he was hearing.

Thomas filled the awkward pause. "Boy, have you changed," he said. "You don't look anything like you did back then. There's that full beard you're sporting, of course. And you've beefed up so much! I should talk, though. I've put on a few pounds myself. Know what I weigh now, Marcel?"

Profett remembered the undisciplined, potato-chip-gorging jerk he'd had the misfortune to bunk with during his last year at Missoula.

Probably 300 pounds, he thought, but he simply said coldly, "I wouldn't venture a guess, but I'm sure you've been eating well."

"You know it," said Thomas, oblivious as usual to the signals being sent. "I hit the scales at two hundred and thirty-eight pounds just this morning."

Dick Thomas had always been a colossal bore, and Profett had no interest in a report on his eating habits, his weight, or anything else about him. However, the man had set alarm bells to ringing loudly in Profett's head. Dick Thomas could do him big damage, and Profett didn't dare brush him off.

"Know how I finally recognized you, Marcel?" Thomas rattled on. "The eyes. When I saw your picture on the jacket of *1999,* I knew I'd seen those eyes somewhere. And then when I heard your voice today on the radio, I finally figured out it was you, Marcel. Took me a while, though.

"Anyhow, like I said, I'm glad to see you got your life all straightened out and are doing so well. What do you say we get together? I'd love to hear your story."

Profett smiled in order to force some warmth into his voice while he tried to figure out what to do. "So it's Dick Thomas. Imagine! It's been years! What are you doing these days?"

"Yeah, it's me all right," said Thomas brightly, "in the flesh. Okay, you want the whole truth? I'm interested in more than just hearing your story. I want to write it for a major Christian periodical."

"You're a writer now?"

"Yeah, isn't that a hoot?" Thomas paused. "I'm not a famous book author like you, of course, but I've had a few things published. And this story would be a sure thing. With your name recognition and my knowledge of your background, I can't miss. I figure I'll use kind of a Paul Harvey slant: 'And now you know the rest of the story.' Clever, huh?"

You big stupid ox, thought Profett. *Why in the world do you think I took a new identity?* "Look, Dick," he said patiently, "I appreciate your interest, but I'd rather not everyone knew the rest of my story. I'm not exactly proud of some things in my past. You understand."

"Of course, old buddy, but, you know, secrets have a way of coming out whether we want them to or not, especially when a guy gets as prominent as you are. If I write your story, it'll be told sympathetically. If somebody else does it—well, the phrase *hatchet job* springs to mind."

Profett was silent for a long moment. "You're going to write this story whether I cooperate or not, aren't you?"

"I was hoping I wouldn't have to make that decision," said Thomas.

You miserable creep, thought Profett. *Intimidate me, will you?* Feigning resignation, he sighed. "Well, okay, I guess if it has to come out, I'd rather it be from a trusted friend like you than from some sensation hunter." He could not keep a sarcastic edge from his voice on the "trusted friend" part, but he knew he could count on Thomas to miss anything more subtle than a hurled brick.

"Great!" said Thomas. "When can we get together?"

"Might as well do it right away," said Profett. His mind was honed to a keen edge by the peril he sensed, and he realized he needed more information. "But what's your situation?" he asked. "Do you live here in the area, are you just visiting, or what?

"As of just about a month ago, I live here," said Thomas.

"And what do you do? Besides writing, I mean. Are you pastoring a church in the area? Is your family here with you?"

"No, that's a sad story," said Thomas. "I'm divorced." He paused. "But, hey, I'm getting over it. That's why I moved out here to Portland. You know—fresh start in a new place and all that."

"So, why Portland? You have friends here, or relatives? Where are you living?"

"No, I got nobody," said Thomas, "which is just the way I want it for now. I've gotta get Ramona, my ex, out of my craw before I take up with somebody new."

Profett could hardly believe how beautifully this seemed to be working out. The guy was totally vulnerable. *And some people say there is no God!* he thought. *But I'd still better find out a bit more.*

"So, why Portland?" he asked again.

"Why not Portland?" said Thomas. "I always thought I'd like to live in the Northwest, and so far, in spite of the famous dampness, I love it. So, what about tomorrow—to get together, I mean."

"Tomorrow's fine."

"Good, where shall we meet?"

As if playing a fish, Profett deftly let out some line; he wanted Thomas to think he was calling the shots, controlling the situation. "Well, let's see," Profett said in a thinking-aloud tone. "At a restaurant? But we'll need privacy. And it's going to take a while."

"Maybe I should come to your place," suggested Thomas. "That way I could pick up some color and atmosphere for the story, maybe take some photos."

"Okay, that's good," said Profett, "but my house is a bit remote and hard to find. Tell you what. How about we meet out here at the intersection of Highway 211 and Schieffer Road, and then you can follow me on up to my place."

A few moments later, with the arrangements made and the time set, Profett hung up the phone. He went directly to his bedstand, opened the drawer, and drew out a shiny, nickel-plated .45 caliber revolver. He checked the cylinder to make sure it was fully loaded. "Dick, Dick," he said, "what a talent you have for bad timing."

At nine the next morning, Profett was waiting in his car at Highway 211 and Schieffer Road when Thomas drove up and parked behind him. Profett jumped from his car and was standing at Dick's door by the time Dick got his seat belt unfastened.

"Hey, Dick, it's good to see you," he said as he thrust his hand out to firmly shake the hand of his old roommate. "Now if you'll just follow me, I'll take you on up to my place." He turned as if to go, then stopped. "You know," he said, "it's such a nice day; if you want, we can stop off at my private spot in the woods where I often go to be alone with the Lord and meditate. You might want to take a picture there—you did say you want atmosphere."

"I'm all yours," said Dick. "Let's go."

Profett returned to his car. *Yes, Dick, old friend,* he thought, *you are all mine.*

After just a short distance, the two turned off Schieffer Road and onto Gray's Hill Road. They passed some houses and a few mobile homes and Christmas tree farms. The road then plunged down a steep hill and up an even steeper one before turning to gravel and then to dirt as it entered a heavily overgrown area.

Profett pulled to a stop at what was little more than a wide spot in the winding muddy road. He got out and walked back to stand beside the lowered driver's window of Thomas's car. "This is it," he said. "What do you think of the place?"

Overhead, the partly cloudy sky showed big patches of blue, and the silence and isolation of the place awed Thomas. "Wow, I can see why you like to come here," he said.

Profett's fingers curled around the handle of the revolver in his coat pocket. *But what if Thomas had told someone where he was going, or whom he was meeting? I can't take that chance.*

"We could begin the interview right here," Profett suggested.

"Okay," agreed Thomas. "Then, we'll get a few photos here and at your house, and that should do it. Get in."

As Profett settled in on the passenger side, Thomas fiddled with a small cassette tape recorder he had brought along for the interview.

"Let's chat a few minutes before you turn that thing on," said Profett. "Kind of get reacquainted."

"So, how are you getting along living all alone?" he continued. "Must be kind of lonely for a guy who's been married. Like this morning. You had breakfast at home alone and then came out here? Or do you eat out?"

"Living alone is no fun," agreed Thomas, "and I do eat out a lot, but not for breakfast. It's easier to just have a bowl of cold cereal with a banana. Do you know how many kinds of cold cereal there are now? You could eat a new one every day of the month and never repeat. I like the old standards best, though; this morning I had Frosted Mini-Wheats.

"But I guess you know all about living alone, Marcel. I assume you've never married, right?"

Profett nodded almost imperceptibly.

"It'd be a pretty strange marriage if you did," said Thomas. "Tell me, what part of all that business about your past was true and what was rumor?" As he talked, he reached down and punched the record buttons on his machine.

"Look," said Profett, "you tell me what you know or think you know from the old days, and I'll tell you what part of it was true."

"Okay," said Thomas. "What I know for sure is that you got kicked out of school in your senior year. The rest was all rumor, and there was plenty of that—most of it pretty bizarre.

"Let's see, as I recall, one story was that you were gay, and that was why you had no use for the women. Personally, I never believed that. Like I told everybody at the time, 'C'mon, if he was gay, who'd be more likely to know it than me? I live with the guy. Not once have I caught him ogling me in the shower or anything like that.' "

"Well, thank you for that heartfelt defense," said Profett sarcastically.

"You're welcome," said Thomas. "The other rumors? Well, according to one story, you were just royally screwed up by your mother. She supposedly had hounded you from the time you were a toddler. 'Make me proud. Live up to your greatness. Don't disappoint me like your miserable, worthless father has. Watch out for loose women.'

"Then there was the weirdest rumor of all, that they sent you home because you had flipped out and thought you were the Antichrist. Wowweeee!

"So, that's what I know. Now you tell me the straight scoop. What actually happened?"

Profett fingered the safety on the gun in his pocket. It had burned him up that he was going to have to do this. It was too up-close, too risky, and too much on the spur of the moment. He liked to plan things meticulously, well in advance, and stay away from the actual dirty work.

But to his surprise, he was now finding it almost electric to be in on the action. And it would be even more exciting if he seized this opportunity to tell someone, even a dope like Dick Thomas, what was actually transpiring under everyone's nose.

"Did you say you heard me for the first time on 'Countdown' only yesterday?" Profett asked.

"Yeah," said Thomas. "You're good."

"Then, maybe you don't know what people are saying about me now," said Profett. "They are saying that I'm Elijah. Now, Dick, it's not by accident that people are thinking that way; it's part of a plan. Now tell me, Dick, who is going to believe I'm Elijah after you get through?"

Thomas laughed. "You must be kidding. That's pretty ridiculous with or without my story. You? Elijah?" He laughed again, but then noticed Profett was not smiling.

"Come on," said Thomas, pleading now. "You can't really think you're Elijah. That's as bizarre as if you really had thought you were the Antichrist back when you got kicked out of Bible college."

"And did you hear why I thought I was the Antichrist?"

"I heard you had a whole list of reasons, all of 'em crazy."

"That's right," said Profett, his eyes gleaming. "I had a whole list of reasons for thinking I was the Antichrist, but you pathetic fools never knew half of them.

"I was born for greatness," said Profett, "unlike you bunch of ninnies I had to put up with in Missoula. I did learn one thing there, though. My destiny was to be evil. Evil and great.

"Do you know what the last piece of evidence was, Dick, what finally convinced me beyond all doubt of my true identity? It was something I'd been living with unwittingly from the day of my birth. Something my dear parents gave me in their total ignorance. Marcel Tyrone Thorpe they named me. Count the letters, Dick Thomas. Six—six—six."

Thomas drew a quick breath. "The number of the Antichrist!" he said.

"No, you fool. Can't you get anything right? It's not just the number of the Antichrist; it is the number of his name."

In a flash Profett had his .45 pointed at Thomas. "Get out of the car," he ordered.

"This is insane," cried Thomas. "If you are the Antichrist, why are you playing Elijah, calling people to repentance, and telling everyone Christ is coming soon?"

"Get out of the car," Profett repeated. He followed as Thomas stumbled out the door, keeping his gun carefully trained on him.

"But why?" cried Thomas. "Why the Elijah thing?"

"Don't you think I know you're playing for time with your stupid questions?" asked Profett. "But I am going to answer them anyhow. You've put me to a lot of trouble, showing up like this out of nowhere, and if I have to deal with you, I'm at least going to have the pleasure of telling you my plan.

"Try to follow, will you? I know it's hard given your, what shall we say, *diminished capacity*"—the voice dripped acid—"but maybe this will help you focus." He waved the gun. "Surely even you can appreciate at least a little the delicious irony of my plan. Who better to use to elevate the Antichrist to prominence than stupid Christians? Don't you see? And all the time they think they are using me. All of them from my egotistical fraud-hunting manager to my status-seeking publisher; they think they are using me.

"Why aren't you laughing, Dick Thomas? Can't you see the humor, the absolute irony? But, of course, probably not, since the only reason you're here is because you want to use me too, just like the rest.

"Well, die happy, man. At last you have some significance. You get to be a symbol of the whole church." With that, Profett fired one shot through Thomas's heart. He then walked to the prostrate form and fired one shot through the temple.

Profett dragged the body off the roadside and into the thick brush. "Out here and at this time of year, nobody will find you before spring," he said, "and by that time there'll be nothing left but a few scattered bones."

He walked back to the car, thinking of the best place to abandon it.

"So long, old friend," he called over his shoulder.

26

D iane! What are you doing there?" David asked, surprised
that she answered his phone call home.

"I'm staying here a couple of days with Mother," said
Diane. "She hasn't been very well."

"What's the matter with her?"

"She's depressed mostly, I guess. She hardly seems able to function
and Dad's so busy. It's a problem."

"Hmmm, that must be why I'm not getting any reaction out of
them."

"Reaction? To what?"

"You haven't heard? I'm dropping out of Multnomah."

"No, David! Why would you do anything so stupid? Does Dad
know about this?"

"He should. I called Mother a couple of days ago and told her about
it. I figured I'd hear back from Dad pretty fast, but so far, not a word.
I guess it's okay with them. Anyhow, I've made up my mind."

"But why? What are your plans? Or don't you have any?"

"I have plans, but I don't have to explain them to you."

"I'm sorry, David. You're right, you don't. But I really would like
to know."

"Okay, since you put it like that. Rick and I are going into the
woodcutting business."

"Rick? I thought he was in the army. The last I heard, you were thinking you should have enlisted when he did."

"Yeah, well, now he's getting out. Too many rules and regulations. Like Multnomah. We're going to be our own bosses, work in the great outdoors, cut firewood when we want to and take off when we feel like it. It'll be great!"

Diane measured her words. She figured the great Rick-and-David woodcutting caper had about as much chance of success as Linus had of giving up his blanket, but she had more pressing matters on her mind right now. Her brother needed to know what was happening at home. "David," she said, "we need to talk."

"Duh, we *are* talking. What other intelligent remarks do you want to make?"

"I'm worried about Dad and Mother, David. Dad is so wrapped up with Profett that he has no time for anything or anyone else, including Mother."

"Well, what do you expect me to do about it? Profett and Dad and Mother are all good Christians, aren't they? They should work it out."

"Yes, they should, but they haven't, and things are really getting serious." She hesitated. "Dad told me that I—that I—" Her voice broke and she began to cry.

David said nothing, and Diane knew she was embarrassing him. "I'm sorry," she said, struggling to regain her composure. "Just because I tried to help the situation, Dad said I have a rebellious 'Jezebel' spirit. And then he hung up on me, and—and—it's a mess, David."

"You? A rebellious spirit? What bull! Hmmph, I never figured Dad would go fanatic on us. Maybe it's good I'm quitting school and moving back home for a while—give the place a little balance."

Diane didn't see how adding a careless son to a fanatical father and a depressed mother made for balance, but she mumbled something about hoping so and added, "Grandpa Brown will be home soon, too. Maybe he can help straighten things out." *At least I'll have someone to talk to,* she thought, *someone I can have confidence in.*

*   *   *

A van stopped in front of the Sheridan Office Complex, the words

"Flowers Unlimited" emblazoned on its door. A man got out carrying a bouquet of dark red roses. He checked the building directory, then ambled down the hall to the door marked "John Profett Ministries." He entered and announced, "Flowers for Miss Shelly Green."

"Oh, they're beautiful!" Shelly proclaimed as she accepted them. She pulled the card from its little envelope and read: "For services above and beyond the call of duty." It was signed, "John Profett and Matt Douglas."

She arranged the flowers just right in a vase, then carried it to the door of Matt's office, knocked, and walked in. "Thank you for the beautiful roses," she said when Matt looked up from his work. "It was sweet of you to send them." She walked to his desk and displayed the roses, turning the vase so he could get the full effect.

"Hey, those are nice, and you deserve them," said Matt, smiling. "John and I want you to know that you are appreciated."

Shelly looked quizzically at Matt. "You know," she said, "Mr. Profett doesn't seem like the 'send roses' type. While you, on the other hand . . ."

Matt blushed.

"You ordered them, didn't you?"

"Well, one of us had to do the actual ordering," Matt admitted.

"I'll bet Mr. Profett doesn't even know about it."

Matt squirmed and didn't answer, so Shelly with a big smile quickly added, "Anyhow, I'm pretty sure I know whose idea it was. Thanks, Matt." She leaned down and kissed him on the cheek, then turned and floated out the door and back to her desk.

Matt returned immediately to his work, but after a moment he paused and looked at the door through which Shelly had just exited. *Wow,* he thought, *has she always smelled that good, or is she wearing new perfume?*

✳   ✳   ✳

Across town in a spotless and well-appointed apartment, the medical examiner was shaking his head as he prepared to have the body removed. "No, it doesn't look like homicide to me, either," he said to the detective handling the investigation. "As you say, there's no sign of a struggle, no evidence of forced entry, no marks on the body. Most likely a suicide. My guess is we'll find she died of an overdose of these." He pointed to an empty prescription bottle on the table nearby. "Can't be sure, of course, until we do an autopsy. I'll let you know what we find. Who was she, again?"

"She was a professor from that seminary out in the university district, a Dr. Elaine Newman. In some kind of trouble, apparently. She'd been suspended from teaching. Something about sexual abuse of students. I guess she liked to dance, but when it came time she couldn't pay the fiddler."

*   *   *

Late that same afternoon, Matt took a call. "I'm Gordon Dennis," the voice said, "Regional Manager for Columbia Pacific. Our corporation president, Mr. Ross Plowman, is here in the city today, and he would like to meet with you and Mr. Profett this afternoon. Can you be here before five?"

"Well, no, I'm afraid that's quite impossible," said Matt, thinking what a lot of nerve the man had to make such a request. "Mr. Profett is out of town, but perhaps we can make an appointment for another time. May I ask what this is concerning?"

"Certainly. I realize that asking you to come down here today is a bit presumptuous," said Dennis. "But if you find it at all possible, I'm sure you'll be glad you put everything else aside.

"Mr. Plowman has been hearing the radio programs featuring you and Mr. Profett, and he's quite taken by them. I can't speak for him, of course, but I can tell you that he likes to make significant contributions directly to ministries he considers particularly worthy.

"I can also tell you that the forest products business has been extremely profitable lately, and with the end of the year approaching Mr. Plowman is likely to be quite generous."

"I see," said Matt. "I certainly would like to accommodate you, but, as I said, Mr. Profett is away. I do expect him back tomorrow. Could we—"

"Mr. Plowman is flying back to Vancouver this evening," Dennis interrupted. "If Mr. Profett is not available, perhaps you could come. Mr. Plowman would prefer to meet you both, but he did say he could talk with either of you."

"Certainly, then," said Matt. "I'll come right down." He got directions, then hung up the phone. He pulled out his briefcase and tossed in a new autographed copy of *1999*, a list of the stations carrying "Countdown," and copies of the latest promotional brochure.

He stopped at Shelly's desk on his way out. "Pray for me," he said. "I'm off to see a big industrialist from out of town who's interested in making a contribution to the cause. Let's hope I impress him as well in person as we apparently did on the radio."

"I will," she said, waving him out the door. "If anybody can do it, you can."

✳ * ✳

The Columbia Pacific offices occupied the entire fourteenth floor of the Frasier Building in downtown Portland. The walnut-paneled halls and bronze-lettered doors clearly said money, and Matt dashed into the men's room to be sure his appearance was its best before meeting this high-powered executive, Mr. Ross Plowman.

When Matt presented himself at the manager's office, the receptionist said, "Oh, yes, Mr. Douglas. Mr. Plowman is expecting you. Please go right in."

Matt rapped on the heavy door, then opened it and stepped inside. The man who came from behind the desk to greet him wore a plaid flannel shirt, jeans, and a denim jacket. He looked for all the world like he had just come in from the woods, and Matt almost expected to see sawdust on his clothes. His build was wiry and his face weathered, and when they shook hands Matt noticed his grip was firm like that of a man who had spent countless hours wielding an axe or a chainsaw. He looked to be about sixty years old.

They sat down on a couch, and Plowman shoved the remnants of a sausage and tomato pizza across the coffee table toward Matt. "Here, son," he said, "have a slice. I'd love to take you out for a nice big steak, but Mrs. Plowman would skin me alive if I ate dinner before I got home. She's having spare ribs tonight, seven-thirty sharp, and I gotta be there, *with* an appetite."

"Dinner at seven-thirty?" echoed Matt, "and you live in British Columbia? You'll never make it. You should be leaving for the airport now."

"Oh, I'll make it all right. Ever hear of a helicopter, my boy? Let's see, now, what time is it?" He glanced at his wristwatch. "Ten past five. I'd say we've got thirty minutes or so to get acquainted, son. Don't wanna cut it too close. Gotta have time to wash up before dinner."

"Well, sir," Matt began, "I understand you are interested in John Profett Ministries. You've heard our program 'Countdown'?"

"I've heard it, and I like it," said Plowman. "It's high time preachers were calling people back to the old ways. Repentance, that's what we need. That's what my daddy preached and that's what I believe."

"Your father was a minister?"

"Fire and damnation, yes! He preached the old-fashioned gospel in logging camps all over British Columbia. He was a man, not a sissy, soft-living, sob-sister like most of these 'reverends' we've got nowadays."

He paused and looked Matt in the eye. "Son," he said, "do I look like a rapist to you?"

Matt swallowed a mouthful of pizza and stammered an answer, "Why I—I don't know," he said. "What does a rapist look like? I mean, no, you don't. Of course not."

"That's what one of them 'reverends' called me. He said I was a forest rapist 'cause I cut down trees. Crazy!" He paused, then raised one eyebrow. "Do you think cuttin' trees makes a man a rapist?"

Matt squirmed. He knew what Plowman wanted to hear. He wanted to be exonerated for his logging practices whether they had been environmentally responsible or not. Matt could almost feel his chances for a big contribution slipping away.

"Well, sir, I think we have to strike a balance. We have to take care of our environment, but people's jobs are important too. In fact, I believe people must come first!" He was perspiring and watching Plowman anxiously to see what the man's reaction would be.

"Balls of fire, son, don't take it so hard!" Plowman pulled a check from his shirt pocket and handed it to Matt. "I wrote this out before you came down here. I've heard you enough to know you're not one of them crazies."

Matt glanced at the check. It said pay to the order of John Profett Ministries the sum of . . . he could scarcely believe it: a one followed by five zeros.

*   *   *

A few minutes later, Matt was in his car headed out of the downtown area and reveling over the check he carried in his wallet. This business of directing John Profett Ministries was certainly proving every bit as exciting as he had hoped. No, that was an understatement; it was thrilling! He had finally been given a key role to play in a drama of real significance. And, if he did say so himself, he was playing that role very well. John Profett Ministries and the Elijah Project were exploding under his guidance.

Matt glanced at his dashboard clock: nearing six-thirty. No wonder he was getting hungry. One slice of pizza had been only an appetizer. He pulled into a Burgerville, where he knew they served halibut for their fish and chips. He thought of the irony of it—a man with $100,000 in his pocket eating at a fast-food joint. But then he commended himself. God's money and God's work were safe in his hands. He would keep the common touch and he would use the Lord's money prudently no matter how much he had. No doubt that was one reason God had chosen him.

A few minutes later as he sat eating in a booth, he thought about how, in the old days, he'd have been eating dinner at home about now. Afterward, he'd have sat around watching TV or just relaxing with Priscilla, resting up for another day at good old KOCB. *How could I have stayed in that nothing job for so long,* he wondered. About the best he could say for it now, looking back, was that it had been honest work and, he supposed, somewhat useful to somebody.

"Useful," he said aloud, "but so ordinary." Now with Profett all that had changed. "How sweet it is!" he exulted.

The thought occurred to him as he left the Burgerville that he could go straight home. He could spend this evening with Priscilla, like an ordinary man. He quickly dismissed the idea. Opportunities awaited him at the office. He was receiving more letters and invitations, more proposals to advance the Elijah Project than he could handle.

Besides, it wasn't that much fun to be around Priscilla these days. One would think that being home all day she would at least have time to clean the house and care for her personal appearance, but she didn't seem to. Yes, she had been traumatized, but how long was she going to milk this thing?

His mind went ahead of him to his office. Shelly was almost as excited about their work as he was and she would probably still be there, working late as usual. Shelly would never let herself go like Priscilla had. Shelly was such an even-tempered person, always cheerful, always smiling, always helpful. What a woman!

He remembered her kiss on the cheek, felt again the warmth of her nearness, smelled the enchanting fragrance of her perfume. Something these past few days—even before the kiss—had made Matt think perhaps she was coming on to him. Her warmer-than-ever smile, her bending close to him at his desk, her frequent incidental touches, the occasional brush of her hand on his. Maybe he was imagining things, but he didn't think so.

Perhaps it's time to find out, Matt thought. Maybe this evening before she left for the night, he would stand close and see whether she moved away or even closer.

And if she moved closer?

He wouldn't plan beyond that point. Who knew? Maybe they would both let nature take its course. Nothing planned. One of those things that sometimes just happen. His heart was beating faster now and his mouth felt dry.

Matt parked in front of the Sheridan Complex and then stopped by the kiosk in the lobby on his way through and bought some breath mints. On the way to his office, he tore open the package and popped one in his mouth.

At the office door, Matt swallowed the lump in his throat, grasped the doorknob, and pushed. The door wouldn't open. Locked. Could Shelly have gone for the day or had she just locked the door for security? Actually, having the door locked was not a bad idea. He wouldn't want anyone walking in on them.

Matt dug out his key and unlocked the door. "Shelly," he called. He listened but there was no answer. He walked to her desk, bent down, and smelled the roses. He pulled out her chair and noticed a pair of high heeled shoes under the desk. He could almost feel her presence, but—

Matt walked into his own office, sat down at his desk, and picked up a small stack of envelopes. Each one contained some proposal or invitation he had thought promising. He shuffled the envelopes, selected one, and took out the letter inside but didn't unfold it. He sighed, rocked back in his chair, then arose and went to Shelly's door, where he stood studying her empty desk and chair for a few moments. He returned to his desk and put away his mail. Then he turned out the lights, locked the door and left.

For a while Matt drove aimlessly. At length he found himself on Sandy Boulevard. This was the area, he'd heard, where prostitutes were a major problem. He drove slowly, scanning the sidewalks. *Where are all these brazen women?*

He cruised the boulevard in one direction and then the other. Nobody. As he left the area he accelerated to normal driving speed. He would never have picked one up anyhow, of course. He wasn't that stupid. Some time later Matt drove into the driveway of his darkened house. Diane would be back in Newberg by now, and Priscilla was already in bed, he assumed; that was the usual situation when he arrived home these days.

Matt went in and quietly prepared for bed without turning on the bedroom light. He crawled in between the sheets and turned on his side away from Priscilla.

He was almost asleep—his last thoughts of Shelly—when he was roused by the ringing of the telephone. Since the phone was on Priscilla's nightstand, Matt waited for her to answer it. When she didn't, he rose up in bed to reach across her. Where she should have been, he felt only empty space. *What the*—Matt thought. He fumbled for the light and turned it on. Priscilla was not there.

He grabbed the phone. "Hello," he said into the mouthpiece. There was no reply. "Hello," he said again. Silence. Matt held the receiver for a long moment, listening for a voice on the other end or a click indicating the caller had hung up. He heard nothing. "Hello," he said one last time.

That's enough of this, he thought, and slammed down the phone. He rolled out of bed, and went to check the bathroom for Priscilla. She was not there. He padded barefoot into the hall and checked the other bedrooms, his anxiety increasing with every step. They were all empty.

He rushed into the living room and the kitchen, leaving every light on behind him as he went. *This cannot be happening again,* his mind screamed as fear, anger and bewilderment flooded over him once more.

Then he saw the note on the kitchen table:

Matt,

I have taken Priscilla with me. I can't tell you how upset I am at her condition. Or how disappointed I am in you for your neglect. You are going to have to either take care of Priscilla or lose her.

Marshall

P.S. Do not come dashing over to my house in the night. Call tomorrow and arrange a time to talk.

Matt was weak-kneed with relief at learning Priscilla was safe. However, his relief quickly gave way to anger. *How dare he come into my home and take away my wife? And she's just as guilty. The Bible says a woman is to leave her father and mother and be joined to her husband, not go running back home whenever her husband doesn't dote on her just the way she thinks he should.*

Women! he thought angrily. *They're all Jezebels!*

27

Matt's anger over Marshall's intervention in his marriage faded quickly. He wanted to nurse the rage, but he knew with awful certainty that his anger was unjustified. Inexorably the anger seeped away and was replaced by a sense of shame that his behavior had earned such a stinging rebuke. Marshall's words repeated in his mind: *I can't tell you . . . how disappointed I am in you.*

For a long moment he stood there barefooted in his underwear, feeling like a scolded child.

Then the thought came to him like the voice of God. *You are ashamed because your father-in-law is displeased with you. What about your Father in heaven? You aren't so concerned about his displeasure.*

"I am too!" Matt argued. "Pleasing him means everything to me—I'm devoting my whole life to his work. And paying an awful price in the process."

Oh, sure you are, the accusing voice said. *But tonight the only reason you didn't commit adultery was because the opportunity wasn't there.*

Matt wanted to argue that point, too. Since the opportunity never presented itself, no one really knew what would have happened if it had. Maybe when it came right down to it, he would not have yielded to the temptation.

Oh, come on! Give me a break! the inner voice replied. *At least retain a little bit of the old Matt's honesty. You know very well what Jesus said: lusting after a woman is sinful even if you don't commit the act.*

Matt hung his head and, note in hand, slowly trudged back into the bedroom. Exhausted, he crawled in between the covers of his lonely empty bed and tried to fall asleep.

It was no use. Every time he closed his eyes, he saw his angel. The little fellow had his face buried in his hands, and he was weeping his eyes out.

"Oh, God, what have I done?" Matt groaned.

✳   ✳   ✳

Matt woke up with gray morning light filtering through the blinds. He knew it was past time to be about the day's business, but he didn't care. This was without doubt going to be his day of reckoning. For a long time he lay in bed, mulling over his failings and grieving over the state to which he and his family had fallen.

He would have much preferred to be angry, so for a while he tried again to blame Marshall for his pathetic situation. It wouldn't wash. He knew that all Marshall had done was make him face the issue. As Marshall's blunt note had said, Matt was going to have to "either take care of Priscilla or lose her."

He relived the heart-stopping moment last night when he had discovered Priscilla missing. To think, he had almost gone to sleep without even realizing she was absent from their bed. How symbolic of the deterioration of their marriage! A deterioration that was all his fault.

Matt picked up the note from his nightstand and read it again. His eyes fixed on the words "how disappointed I am in you for your neglect."

It's true, he thought. *I let her down when she needed me most.*

And when Diane had tried to warn him, he had savagely turned on her, too. He had called his sweet daughter a Jezebel, and hung up the phone on her. How could he have done it? She had only wanted to warn him.

He remembered the dream in which he had publicly humiliated Diane. "Out of character for me," he had said. "I would never treat anyone that way," he had said.

That dream had revealed his potential for misusing people, but he hadn't heeded that warning either. *I've offended my own dear daughter. How could I be so blind?*

He wiped his teary eyes on the pillowcase. He wanted to ask God to forgive him, but he knew there was more on his plate than his shabby treatment of Priscilla and Diane.

There was this business with Shelly. Last night he had left Priscilla at home alone while he went lusting after Shelly. In more than twenty years of marriage, he had never been unfaithful to Priscilla. And to think that he would have betrayed her now with Shelly, who at the bottom line meant nothing to him.

An incident from the Old Testament came to Matt's mind. One of Judah's more godly kings failed when God left him on his own to show him what was in his heart, or something like that.

Matt dragged himself out of bed and into his office. He took a concordance from his bookshelf and located the passage: 2 Chronicles 32:31. Matt sat down in his desk chair, took his Bible, and looked up the verse. The king was Hezekiah, and the text read, "God left him to test him and to know everything that was in his heart."

Matt's eyes again filled with tears. God had left him on his own to test him and he had miserably failed the test. He didn't deserve Priscilla. He didn't deserve Diane and David. And he certainly didn't deserve to head up John Profett Ministries.

What an irony that he should be responsible for the Elijah Project, calling people to repentance in preparation for the return of Christ! A wretch like him calling other people to holiness! What hypocrisy! It would be a wonder if God didn't strike him dead.

Matt rose from his desk and trudged into the bathroom. His image in the bathroom mirror looked more like a skid-row bum than a Christian executive. His eyes were bleary, his cheeks and chin were covered with stubble, his hair was a fright, and his robe hung open over his underwear.

Oh, God, Matt prayed, *You are a holy and righteous God, who will not punish the righteous for the sins of the guilty. I know I deserve whatever comes to me, but spare me, Lord, for Priscilla's sake, for Diane's and David's sakes, for John Profett's.*

Matt didn't really feel like his prayer for mercy had been heard, but whether it had or not, his choices were now clear. He would go to each of those he had sinned against and beg forgiveness, starting with Priscilla.

Profett was due back in town today, and Matt would tell him everything as well. Of course, he would submit his resignation—and it would surely be accepted. Matt remembered how passionately Profett had implored Priscilla to quit work so as not to compromise his ministry. What Matt had done was a hundred times worse—no, ten thousand times worse—than Priscilla working. Profett would not want Matt associated with him any more, and he would be absolutely right about that.

Matt returned to his office and telephoned Marshall's residence. When Marshall answered, Matt breathed a quick prayer for God's help. "It's me," he said, "Matt." He didn't want Marshall to tear into him or to think he was going to excuse himself at all, so he quickly added, "I'm sorry you had to come home to such a disaster, and I know it's all my fault. I love Priscilla. I know I haven't showed it by my behavior, but I really do love her, and I'm sorry. I'm *so sorry!*" His voice was husky but Matt managed to keep it from breaking.

"I'm sorry, too," said Marshall. "But sorry isn't enough. There are going to have to be some changes, Matt. Priscilla needs attention and care—more than you seem willing to give her."

"I know," said Matt. "But I *am* willing to give her the attention she needs. I am! Please believe me."

"And what about your job? You can't spend twelve, fifteen, eighteen hours a day working for Profett and still have the time and energy you need for Priscilla."

"I'm resigning my job," said Matt. "I plan to tell Profett today."

"You're resigning?" said Marshall, surprise registering in his voice.

"But I thought you were totally committed to Profett."

"I'm not fit for a high calling like that," said Matt. "God put me to the test and I failed. It's all over for me as far as doing anything great for God is concerned."

"That sounds to me like self-pity talking," said Marshall, "but I'll tell you what. Call again *after* you're terminated with Profett. Then perhaps Priscilla will listen to what you have to say about a future for the two of you."

*   *   *

Slowly, mechanically, Matt showered, shaved, and dressed. He was just tying his shoelaces when the phone rang. The voice sounded familiar but he couldn't place it at first. "Oh, yes, Captain Drake," said Matt dully, after the caller identified himself.

"We need to talk," said Drake. "There have been some new developments related to the kidnapping of Mrs. Douglas. Do you suppose you could come down to my office at the East Precinct?"

"New developments?" said Matt. "Does that mean you know who did it? I didn't suppose there was much chance you would ever find those creeps."

"As a matter of fact, we do have a man in custody whom we believe to have been involved."

"Good, but I really don't think there's anything more I can tell you. And I am awfully busy right now."

"I'm sorry to impose on your time, Mr. Douglas, but it is important that I talk with you as soon as possible. Could you come down right away?"

"Well, yes, I suppose I could if you really feel it's necessary, but—"

"I'll be waiting," said Captain Drake.

*   *   *

As he hung up the phone, Drake turned to a fellow officer. "He's coming," he said. "Now we'll see what happens when we rattle his cage."

*   *   *

Matt arrived at the Portland Police Bureau East Precinct still feeling beaten. It was bad enough that his life had practically fallen apart but now he had to endure this additional drain on his time and energy, probably for nothing.

"How are you?" Drake said, extending his hand as Matt entered his office. Drake indicated a chair for Matt to sit in, then sat down himself in the wooden swivel chair behind his desk. "What do you hear from Marshall?" Drake asked. "Is he back yet from his trip to Europe?"

"Just got home yesterday," said Matt, glossing over his chaotic home situation. "In fact, I haven't even seen him yet."

"And Mrs. Douglas, how is she doing?"

"Not as well as I had hoped," said Matt. "She can't seem to get over what happened." *Enough of the small talk,* thought Matt. *I'm sure he didn't ask me down here to catch up on my family.* "You say you have a man in custody? What's the story, and how can I help?"

"We do have a suspect and he has admitted his involvement," said Drake.

"Good, good, and has he identified the others?"

"The man we have in custody is charged in a series of crimes," explained Drake. "He is cooperating with us, hoping to get a reduced sentence, and he has identified one accomplice. We have a warrant out for the man's arrest, but it appears he may have left the area. The suspect in custody doesn't know the name of the third man directly involved, but we hope to identify him in due time."

"Great work!" said Matt, thankful for at least one glimmer of good news in an otherwise dark time. "I'm extremely pleased! And maybe this will lift Priscilla's spirits a little, too."

"You may remember," said Drake, "that I surmised at the time that the kidnapping of Mrs. Douglas was a crime of opportunity, that she just happened to be in the wrong place at the wrong time."

"Yes, I remember," said Matt.

"The man we have in custody says that was not the case. He insists that Mrs. Douglas was targeted specifically."

Matt felt a rising fear over the implications of Drake's remark. "But why?" he said. "Why would they do that?"

"He says they were hired for the job."

"Hired? By whom?"

Drake looked him straight in the eye and sprang his trap. "He says by *you*, Mr. Douglas. You hired them to kidnap your wife and told them their payoff would be the car she was driving—as well as her personal favors. You in effect told them they could rape your wife."

"That's a lie!" said Matt jumping to his feet. "Why would I do anything like that?"

Drake held his piercing gaze on Matt. "Please sit down, Mr. Douglas," he said.

"It doesn't make any sense!" stormed Matt, staying on his feet. "Surely you are not going to take the word of a criminal about something like this."

"Please *sit down*, Mr. Douglas," Drake repeated sternly.

Matt slowly settled back onto the edge of his chair.

"I have been asking the same question you asked," Drake said. "Why would an upstanding man such as yourself do a thing like that? I can't imagine it, but I've been around police work long enough to know that stranger things have happened."

"Maybe so," said Matt defiantly, "but not in this case. It plain didn't happen."

Drake drummed his fingers on his desk. "I have another *why* question, Mr. Douglas. Why would the man we have in custody say you were behind this crime? I don't understand that, Mr. Douglas. What would he have to gain by lying to us?"

"That's why I asked you here. I need your help in solving this dilemma." His voice was smooth, almost oily.

"There's nothing I can do," said Matt, "except tell you once and for all that I had no prior knowledge and no participation of any kind in my wife's kidnapping."

Drake stroked his chin. "As a matter of fact," he said, as if thinking of it for the first time, "there is one thing you could do. You could take a polygraph test. It would be voluntary, you understand. I can't require it, but it would certainly help put my mind at rest. Assuming, of course, that you pass it."

"A lie detector? You want me to take a lie detector test?" Matt asked. He shook his head in bewilderment. "I don't know.

"Wait a minute! Why should I be the one? Why don't you test this criminal who's telling you these fantastic stories? He's the one you should have on your polygraph."

"I thought you might feel that way," said Drake. "That's why I have already asked him to take the polygraph." Drake paused like a cat playing with a mouse. "He passed it."

Drake let that news sink in for a moment, then arose from his chair to come and stand over Matt. "And you, Mr. Douglas?"

Matt sat stunned. His mind reeled as imaginary sirens sounded and red lights flashed in his brain. He shook his head trying to clear it enough to think rationally. All he knew was that he was in terrible danger, and he called on his instincts to take over. *Be calm. Don't make a rash decision. When in doubt, delay until you see your way clearly.*

"I'll have to get back to you on that," Matt said, his voice sounding calm and totally unlike he felt.

"I'll be waiting," said Drake.

*   *   *

Matt drove away from the East Precinct with his mind in a whirl. One question Drake had raised truly perplexed him. Why would the confessed kidnapper have implicated Matt? What motive could he have for lying? It made no sense.

There's only one explanation, thought Matt. *This is God's retribution.*

28

att! Good morning! How are you?" John Profett was obviously feeling good. So good that he did not seem to notice how sober Matt was and how haggard he looked. He also did not bother to inquire why Matt had come into the office late.

"As a matter of fact, I—uh—" Matt began, but Profett interrupted.

"They love us in Tampa Bay," he said, leaning back in his comfortable office chair. "I want to set up a southeast base of operations there as soon as possible. And in Detroit I've recruited a man who's really sharp. His name's Don Davison, but I call him my Detroit Matt because he can do in that area the same kind of fantastic job you've done here.

"Of course, you'll be in charge of it all. How soon can you get out to organize an office in Tampa? After you do that, and get Detroit started, we need to get our overseas operations going. Australia and England both look like hot prospects."

He paused and grinned at Matt. "Exciting, isn't it?"

"It certainly is," said Matt, "which makes it all the harder to tell you—there's a problem here at home."

"A problem? Always!" said Profett. "But we're nearly unstoppable now. If there's a problem, we'll deal with it."

"This is a personal problem," said Matt, looking at the floor. "It breaks my heart to have to tell you this, but—" he raised his eyes to face Profett squarely—"I've let you down. I've failed you, and I've failed God, and I'm not fit to continue in this ministry."

Profett's face fell. "Maybe you'd better sit down and tell me what this is all about."

"Priscilla has left me," said Matt, slumping into a chair. "I've alienated not only her but Diane and David as well. There's no point going into the details, but the Bible says a Christian leader must 'manage his own family well' and 'if anyone does not know how to manage his own family, how can he take care of God's church?' I'm simply not qualified for the position of trust you've given me. I'm sorry, but I have to resign."

Profett slowly nodded in understanding. "Your concern for high standards among Christian leaders is admirable. Actually, that is one of the things that qualifies you to hold this job. I wouldn't want a man with no standards." He paused. "Seems to me you should stay on."

"But I've fallen short of the standards," said Matt.

"Of course you have. Nobody's perfect. But tell me, what are the standards for? What is their purpose?"

"Well, they are to protect the integrity of the ministry so as not to bring it into disrepute."

"Exactly. Protecting the ministry is what's important. Especially this ministry at this critical stage. And this ministry needs you, Matt. I'm sure you'd agree that preparing the world for the soon return of Christ is far more important than your family spat."

"Of course," said Matt, "but—"

Matt didn't know whether to tell Profett about Drake's accusations and about lusting after Shelly or not. He hadn't planned to because he saw no point in it. If mismanaging his family disqualified him, why cite other grounds also? But now he didn't know what to do.

"I—I—" he stammered. "I have other problems, too. Problems that could really embarrass you and the ministry. The police are saying I planned Priscilla's abduction. They want me to take a lie detector test. And—and—" he decided not to be specific about Shelly—"God has put his finger on other sins in my life as well."

"Tell me the truth," commanded Profett. "Did you have anything to do with Priscilla's abduction?"

"No! I didn't!" exclaimed Matt.

"I believe you," said Profett. "Since you weren't involved, they will have a real tough time ever proving that you were. My advice is, don't take their little test; they are just fishing. But whatever you decide about that, I want you to know that I believe in you, and I am going to stand by you every step of the way through this thing, Matt."

Matt's eyes filled with tears. "I can't tell you how much I appreciate your trust," he said. "You are a true friend." He wiped his eyes and smiled.

But then his face clouded again. "But I still have a major problem with Priscilla. She hasn't recovered well at all, and she needs my special care and attention. Probably will for some time. In the press of my duties here, I've neglected her, and now I have to make up for it. At the very least I need a leave of absence for a few days, and then I'll need to curtail my schedule to a regular forty-hour week for the foreseeable future."

Profett stared at Matt. "I wonder if you can hear what you are saying? First you want to quit, and then you want a leave of absence. Either way the Lord loses your services on the Elijah Project just when they are most critically needed. Can't you see that Satan is determined to sidetrack you one way or another?"

Matt hung his head. "I can see that," he said, "and believe me, I don't want that to happen. But I don't know what else I can do." His voice had a quality of desperation, and his words invited Profett to play rescuer.

Profett seized the opportunity. "You've got to stand strong, Matt. You should call Satan's bluff, just as you should call the bluff of the police. Both of them are trying to intimidate you."

"But I could lose Priscilla unless I give her special care," said Matt. His eyes pleaded for understanding. "I couldn't endure that."

Profett tossed the pen he'd been holding onto his desk and folded his arms. "Then Satan has got you. Satan always attacks at our weakest point, and he knows your weakest point is Priscilla."

The comment and Profett's self-assured manner irritated Matt. "Priscilla is not my 'weakest point,' " he said. "She is my *wife*."

"Meaning she can't be both? Jezebel was Ahab's wife, too, but she was also his weakest point."

"Priscilla is not Jezebel!" said Matt. "And I am not Ahab! This is a new scene, with a new cast of characters. Why must you harp on Jezebel and Ahab all the time?"

"Okay, forget them," said Profett. "What about Jesus? Is it okay if I harp on him? He said a true disciple has to be willing to lose even wife and children for his sake."

"No," said Matt. "He said we have to put him ahead of father, mother, brothers, sisters, and even our own lives. He didn't include a man's wife in that list."

"Well, now, I think he did," said Profett. "Let's just take a look." He picked up his Bible and turned directly to Luke 14. He scanned the page for a moment, then with raised eyebrows and an air of absolute vindication, he shoved the book in Matt's face. "Read chapter 14, verse 26," he ordered.

Matt took the Bible and read, " 'If anyone comes to me and does not hate his father and mother, his wife and children, his brothers and sisters—yes, even his own life—he cannot be my disciple.' "

"Now, let's see," said Profett. "Did Jesus include wife and children among those we must be prepared to 'hate' for his sake, or not?"

"Okay, I was wrong," said Matt, feeling utterly miserable.

"Look," Matt said after a few moments. "I didn't want to tell you this, but I guess I have to. I can't in good conscience continue in a ministry focused on calling people to repentance. With the sin in my own life, I'd be a hypocrite."

He paused and watched for Profett's reaction. Profett simply waited for the explanation he knew had to follow.

"Last night," said Matt, "I almost committed adultery. Only the grace of God kept me from it, because it was certainly in my heart."

Profett's face was expressionless. "And what have you done just now?"

Confused, Matt shook his head slightly. "Just now? I just now told you that I'm guilty of committing adultery in my heart."

"You have confessed your sin, right?"

"Yes."

"And when we confess our sin, what does God do?"

"He forgives us, but—"

"Now, let's get this straight. Less than twenty-four hours ago you committed adultery in your heart, and now you have confessed it already. Seems to me you've done pretty well. King David committed adultery—literally—and afterward covered it up for months before finally confessing. Yet God didn't disqualify him. In fact, the Bible calls him a man after God's own heart."

Profett shook his head decisively. "I'm sorry, Matt, but you haven't given me one good reason why your greatest days of service on the Elijah Project can't still be ahead of you. Wait, I take back the sorry part. I'm *not* sorry; I'm extremely pleased that there is no reason you cannot continue."

He frowned and looked intensely into Matt's eyes. "Unless, of course, you simply give up."

Matt grimaced but said nothing.

"Look, Matt, I know it's tough being alienated from your family like this. My guess is that if you just hold fast to God's will, he will turn things around for you and bring your family back, not only to you but to his service. If you fail now, not only will the Elijah Project suffer immeasurable harm, but you will be out of God's will for the rest of your life. And so will your family, the very ones you say you care about. Tell me that you won't let that happen, Matt. Tell me."

Matt rubbed his forehead. "I don't know!" he said. "Maybe you're right. I just don't know! Let me think about it and pray about it a while."

"Of course," said Profett. "Take the rest of the day off, but I'm counting on you to be back ready to go full speed ahead tomorrow. Remember what Jesus said, 'No one who puts his hand to the plow and looks back is fit for service in the kingdom of God.' The problems you raised won't destroy you or make you unfit for God's service, but looking back will. Think about it, Matt. Think long and hard."

"I will," said Matt. "Believe me, I will." *Hmmm,* he thought, *Profett certainly doesn't want to let me go. What does it take to disqualify a person in his eyes? Murder?*

29

Matt drove home from his office at the Sheridan Complex with his insides churning. *This is no doubt how people get ulcers,* he thought. He pressed one hand to his stomach just under his rib cage and could almost feel an ulcer forming.

Part of him wanted desperately to seize the reprieve Profett had offered and to continue with the Elijah Project. What sense did it make to write off all he had invested in John Profett Ministries and walk away empty-handed? If he could just stay the course, there seemed practically no limit to where he and Profett could go, nationally and even worldwide.

But if I stay with Profett, I may lose Priscilla forever, Matt thought. He tried to imagine what that would mean but couldn't. All he knew was that when she was gone, like now, his life seemed to lose all meaning. But maybe God was testing him. Profett had said that if he was willing to lose Priscilla for the Lord's sake it would not actually come to that.

On the other hand, how had things ever come to their present sad state? Once—after the kidnapping—he had told himself he had to follow through on this Profett business to learn for sure the truth about the man. For Priscilla's sake, he had to do it. But he had long since lost sight of that purpose. He had been caught up completely in Profett's agenda.

And what about this Shelly thing? Profett had compared Matt favorably with King David, who confessed his adultery only after he was confronted by the prophet Nathan. *Supposedly I've repented more quickly than David did,* thought Matt, *but he came out of his experience singing about the blessings of forgiveness. I don't feel anything remotely like that.*

As he pulled into his driveway, Matt told himself aloud, "Well, you know what to do about that." He remembered his prayer of the previous day. Wallowing in guilt and self-pity, he had asked God to spare him for his family's sake and for John Profett's sake. Now he realized that such a prayer itself needed forgiveness. When God forgave anyone, he did it because Jesus died on the cross for our sins and on no other grounds.

Matt chided himself for his fuzzy thinking about something so basic. *Where is this great, clear-headed, and fearless investigator you pretend to be?* he asked himself. *Isn't it about time you faced some hard questions and got to the bottom of a few things—like your own motives in all of this John Profett business?*

What you need to do, Matt advised himself, *is to fast and pray until you find some answers.*

Matt ignored the painful emptiness of his house and walked immediately down the hall to the room he used as his home office. His hopes began rising even as he entered the room. He felt almost a hush as if in a holy place. The countless hours he had spent here preparing to teach his Sunday-school class and studying for his "Hear and Now" broadcasts served now to hallow it.

Fast and pray. The few times he had set himself to do that had hardly ever made him miss a single meal. Once he became that earnest, answers were never long in coming.

This time was no exception. In little more than an hour of prayer and reflection, he found—not all his answers, certainly—but some definite direction.

One thing became clear: he had been wrong to choose John Profett Ministries over his family. He wanted to rush to Priscilla's side and tell her, to explain how he had been misled and what had now brought him to his senses. He longed to see Diane and David too, to gather them all in his arms, assure them of his love, and ask their forgiveness.

However, something else now demanded his immediate attention. He had evidence—there all the time but only now recognized—that John Profett might be implicated in Priscilla's kidnapping. But unless he proved that, any reconciliation with Priscilla was going to be pretty shaky. How could she trust a husband still considered by the police to be the number one suspect in her kidnapping and rape?

That was probably why Marshall had taken Priscilla away in the first place. Sure, he was shocked at her condition when he returned from his trip, but that was only part of it. Though Drake had pretended to Matt that he didn't know Marshall was back from Europe, the truth was he'd probably told Marshall that Priscilla was in danger living with Matt. He could almost hear Drake: "No, I can't prove anything yet. But if she were my daughter, I'd get her out of there."

What Matt needed now was some way to confirm his suspicions of Profett—or disprove them. But how?

He remembered the glossy book jacket as Profett handed him that new copy of *1999*. When he had quit KOCB, he'd brought the book home and placed it on his shelf, a valued copy personally autographed by the author and inscribed to Matt.

He looked up from his desk to his bookshelf. There it was, still pristine, still covered, no doubt, with Profett's fingerprints. Could the answer to his questions have been sitting here in the room with him all the time?

He grabbed the telephone and called Captain Drake. "I'd like to see you," he said, "right away if possible."

✳   ✳   ✳

An hour later, Drake indicated a chair for Matt to sit in just as he had in the same room not twenty-four hours earlier. "I'm a little surprised to see you," Drake said. "I presume this means you are ready to take the polygraph."

Matt sat on the edge of his chair, a brown paper bag in his lap. "Actually, I've got something else altogether on my mind," said Matt. "In here—" he held up the paper bag—"is something that may shed light on a lot of things." He returned the bag to his lap, tore it open lengthwise and carefully held up a copy of *1999* by the corners.

Drake looked disgusted. "I don't appreciate people who waste my time, Mr. Douglas," he said, rising. "Come back and see me when you're ready to cooperate."

"Wait!" said Matt. "You don't understand. I have reason to believe that John Profett was the one behind the kidnapping of my wife. This book jacket should have a dandy set of his fingerprints on it. This is our chance to find out at last who he really is."

Drake stared deadpan at Matt. "Do you want to know what I think?" he asked. "I think you are trying to point a finger at someone else to divert suspicion from yourself. And Profett is supposed to be your friend."

Drake raised his voice. "Crane!" A very large uniformed policeman immediately opened the office door and stepped inside. "Crane, get this piece of—" He paused and pursed his lips. "Get Mr. Douglas out of here."

Crane took two long steps and seized Matt by the arm, practically raising him out of his chair.

Matt jerked away from him. "Take your hands off of me!" he said, his eyes blazing. "Now, look," he said to Drake. "You are supposed to be an investigator. You should be considering all the evidence. You may not like me, and that's your right, but you have no right to ignore evidence."

Drake's voice fairly dripped acid. "I'm not in the habit of taking advice on investigations from my chief suspect," he said.

We'll never get any place this way, Matt thought desperately. "All right," he said, "you told me to come back when I'm ready to cooperate. I'm ready now. I'll take your polygraph—*if* you'll run a check on these prints."

Drake looked at him, one eyebrow raised.

Matt sensed his indecisiveness. "What have you got to lose? If I'm lying, you will know it, and if Profett is clean, you'll know that too."

"I don't do investigations just because there's 'nothing to lose,' " said Drake. "We operate around here on things like probable cause. Now, what makes you think Profett is implicated? Apart from wanting to clear your own skirts, that is?"

"I got a strange phone call a while back," said Matt. "Didn't think anything of it at the time. A clerk at Allbest Electronix phoned to tell me about a recall on a telephone dialing machine he said I bought there."

Drake waved his hand in a gesture of dismissal. "So?"

"So, I didn't buy any such machine, but apparently somebody using my name did. This afternoon, I got to thinking about that clerk's call and I checked back with him on the date; it was at the same time we were running a telephone survey on KOCB. I remember that John Profett was extremely confident that the yes votes would win, said the Lord had assured him of it. I think he helped the Lord a little.

"Now, if that's true," Matt continued, "and Profett used my name in that scheme, maybe that wasn't the only time. Maybe the kidnapper you have in custody implicated me in Priscilla's kidnapping because Profett hired him using my name."

Drake was now showing signs that he might not dismiss Matt's story out of hand. "I'll need the name of that clerk at Allbest," said Drake. "You realize I'm going to check out every word you say."

"Absolutely," said Matt, undeterred. "If Profett did impersonate me, that would explain why the man you have in custody passed his lie detector test. He truly believed I hired him."

Drake rubbed his chin for a moment, then picked up the phone. "Find me Detective Schulz," he said. "Marilyn," he said a moment later, "I have a gentleman here who wants to take the polygraph. How soon can you test him? Good. Crane will bring him right down."

Drake hung up and turned to Matt. "Give your book to Officer Crane," he said. "Your test will take an hour and a half to two hours. By then, with any luck, we'll have talked to the Allbest clerk, and we will have in hand a copy of Profett's record. If he has one. Then we'll talk again."

"Thank you," said Matt. "You won't be sorry."

"I'm sure *I* won't," said Drake. As Matt followed Crane from the room to his rendezvous with an unfamiliar electronic gadget, he thought, *These things aren't admissible in court and yet I'm trusting my fate to one. Not a real smart thing to do.*

30

Detective Marilyn Schulz was a petite, young-looking woman with short dark hair, who seemed miscast as a police officer. *Not over 115 pounds soaking wet,* Matt thought. *How can she handle murderers and rapists? She looks more like women's-wear help than a skilled interrogator.*

Maybe her appearance was part of her strategy. Disarm your opponent, make him think you are easy. If so, it was not going to work this time. "Never underestimate an adversary," he told himself as she hooked him to the piece of equipment that would now pass judgment on his truthfulness.

The tiny room was plain, bare of decoration, and almost empty. Matt sat in a chair with the polygraph equipment on a small table beside him. Situated slightly behind him and to his left was the only other piece of furniture in the room, a small chair in which his questioner sat, her face out of Matt's view.

"Is your name Matt Douglas," Schulz asked, "and do you live at 16142 S.W. Argay Terrace in Beaverton, Oregon?"

"Yes," said Matt.

"Are you the husband of Priscilla Douglas, and are your two children named Diane and David?"

"Yes."

Matt knew something about what to expect. Schulz had gone over the questions with him ahead of time. There would be ten questions, she explained, and no surprises. There would be mundane questions like the first two with no connection whatever to the kidnapping. Then she would ask the critical questions about his possible involvement.

"Did you talk with anyone about the kidnapping of Priscilla Douglas before it happened?" Detective Schulz asked.

Here it comes, Matt thought. His mouth was dry and he ran the tip of his tongue over lips that felt parched. "No, I did not," he said.

*   *   *

Almost ninety minutes later, Detective Schulz put down her pad, rose from her chair, and began to disconnect Matt from the machine. The test was over.

"So, how'd I do?" Matt ventured with a weak smile.

"The test indicates your answers have been truthful."

Truthful! He had passed! "I was so nervous," Matt said, flexing his fingers and twisting his wrists. "When I'm accused of something, I feel guilty even if I am not. I was afraid you might pick up on that and think I was lying." He paused, then with a big grin he could not restrain, he said, "What a relief!"

"It's natural to be nervous when you're taking the polygraph," said Detective Schulz. "But it's a misunderstanding to think that will affect the results."

"So," Matt ventured again, "I know polygraph results aren't admissible in court. How much validity do you and Drake attach to them?"

"Properly administered, we consider them reliable." She paused, then smiled. "I'd say you are no longer a suspect in your wife's kidnapping."

Matt's spirits soared. Now Priscilla and her father would know he hadn't done it. But what about John Profett? What role had he played?

*   *   *

"Captain Drake will see you now," said Officer Crane as he summoned Matt from the East Precinct waiting room. He escorted Matt down the hall and into the captain's office.

Drake looked up when Matt entered. "So, you passed your polygraph."

His voice was expressionless and Matt couldn't help thinking he seemed disappointed. *Is this guy going to try to hang me anyhow?* Matt wondered.

"Mr. Profett didn't fare quite so well in our check of his prints," continued Drake. Then he seemed to rouse from his preoccupation with "just the facts" to realize that Matt was still standing before his desk like a defendant in front of a judge. "Sit down, sit down," he told Matt, sweeping his hand toward an empty chair. He sounded almost friendly.

Matt dropped, relieved over Drake's apparent change of attitude toward him. At the same time, though, his heart pounded over the news that Profett's prints had turned up something. Was he about to get his second big triumph in one day?

"Mr. Profett is not," said Drake.

Matt blinked his eyes and shook his head at the cryptic statement. Had he missed something? "He's not?" Matt echoed. "Not what?"

"Not a prophet. Not named Profett. Not anything he claims to be."

Crane entered the room again before Drake could elaborate and handed Drake several sheets of paper. Drake gave one to Matt. "Meet Marcel Tyrone Thorpe," he said, "a real sweetheart."

Matt scanned the computer printout Drake had given him and read:

MARCEL TYRONE THORPE

DOB: May 12, 1953, Sandpoint, Idaho

Description: Caucasian male, 5' 9", 172 lbs., stocky build, dark brown hair and eyes, sometimes wears full beard. No distinguishing marks

AKA: John James Johnson, John Wesley Bishop, John Luther Martin, John P. Daniel

Last known address: Shepherd's Glen, Maine (May, 1989)

Arrests:

4/12/74, Bonner County, Idaho, murder, two counts, dismissed

4/12/74, Bonner County, Idaho, arson, dismissed

10/2/76, Kent County, Michigan, fraud, dropped

6/6/78, Boone County, W. Virginia, fraud, dropped

9/26/84, Erie County, New York, arson, dropped

5/8/89, Cumberland County, Maine, fraud and arson, dismissed

As he read the record, Matt's anger grew. This man had evidently been victimizing people all across the country for years and never served time for it. How many broken lives had he left behind? How many Priscillas and Matts had he destroyed?

A terrible fury began to rise somewhere behind Matt's eyeballs. In his mind Matt saw himself lunging down the hall of his home into David's bedroom, drawing out the Luger from the desk drawer, loading it, then charging down the road to the office of John Profett Ministries, finding Profett, and emptying all nine shots into the man's head and chest.

God help me, Matt prayed silently.

When he again managed to speak, Matt's voice was husky with the boiling rage he was fighting to control. "This simply cannot be allowed to continue," he said calmly. "There are even murders on here. Somebody has got to stop this man."

Drake nodded. "The two in Idaho were his own mother and father. Like I said, he's a real sweetheart."

"So what do you plan to do about it?"

Drake shook his head. "Our problem is the same one all those other jurisdictions no doubt faced. We can't prove Profett has done anything. It's mostly just a gut feeling at this point. A feeling and the rather suspicious fact that people who put obstacles in his path tend to meet with serious misfortunes."

"Do they ever! Think of the human suffering," said Matt. "Every item on here"—he waved the rap sheet—"probably represents someone unfortunate enough to get crossways of John Profett. Or Marcel Tyrone Thorpe or whoever you said he really is. And these are only the ones the authorities know about. How many more were there? How many like Dr. Elaine Newman?"

"The medical examiner ruled her death a suicide," said Drake.

"And you believe that?"

Drake raised his eyebrows. "I think we'd better take another look."

Matt shook his head in frustration. "There must be some way to get the goods on him," said Matt. "There just has to be."

Drake nodded. "You know," he said, "with your help we might be able to do it."

"What would you want me to do?" asked Matt. "Whatever it is, I'll do it."

"It's quite simple, really," said Drake. "Just become an obstacle."

Over the next two hours Matt and Drake made meticulous plans to trap Profett. "This guy is as clever as he is ruthless," said Drake, "and we must not underestimate him. That means, among other things, we deal with him in a setting where we control all the variables—like in your house."

He paused and looked to Matt for a response to his implied question.

"Hmmm, I don't know," said Matt. "Ordinarily we would meet at our office at the Sheridan Complex."

Drake persisted. "Tell him Priscilla is back home and not well, and you need him to come to your house to meet with you both."

Matt shook his head. "I don't want him in the same city with Priscilla, much less the same house. I couldn't be responsible for my actions if I saw him near her again. Anyhow, Priscilla has been through enough; I don't want her involved in this."

"You have a better idea, then?"

Matt only frowned and was silent.

"Think it over," said Drake. "If you can devise a better plan—one that doesn't include Priscilla—I'd like to hear about it. Otherwise, why don't you let her decide whether she wants to be involved? Talk it over and let me know what you decide.

"Now, if you want to go ahead, give us time to move in a recorder and surveillance cameras. Then, once we get Profett there, you'll need to pose a threat to him. Suppose you inform him you have decided to resign and are going to tell the media exactly why—because you no longer believe in him or his message."

"That would do it, all right," said Matt. "He goes crazy when he's criticized in the media. That's how Elaine Newman touched him off."

Drake nodded. "While you give Profett the bad news in the living room, a couple of other officers and I will be watching from strategic spots, just to make sure things don't get out of control."

Drake rubbed his hands together, and Matt wasn't quite sure whether he was relishing the chase or nervous about covering all his bases.

"If we do decide to go ahead with this plan," said Matt, "and I'm not saying we will, but if we do, are you satisfied that every contingency would be covered and you'd keep Priscilla safe?"

Drake's eyes narrowed. "I will be satisfied," he said "as soon as I take one more precaution." He picked up his phone. "Crane," he said, "put around-the-clock surveillance on John Profett. I want to know every move he makes—starting immediately, and until further notice."

He hung up and turned to Matt. "*Now* I'm satisfied."

"I'd better get going, then," said Matt, rising to his feet. "I'll let you know one way or the other just as soon as we've reached a decision."

"You're on your way to see Marshall?" asked Drake. "If so, I'll call and assure him that you are no longer a suspect. That ought to help a little bit."

*   *   *

Later that afternoon Marshall himself opened his front door to admit Matt. "Drake called," said Marshall. "He brought us up to date—that you're clear, and Profett is a con man named Thorpe." He paused. "I—we—were really glad to hear that you exposed him, Matt."

He escorted Matt into the living room where Priscilla sat on the couch. She was better groomed than he had seen her in days, though her eyes still lacked their old sparkle. "Hello, Matt," she said.

"Hello, Priscilla. You really look nice."

"I'll leave you two alone to talk," said Marshall as he turned to leave.

"No, please stay," said Matt. "I want you to hear what I have to say. It's important to me that both of you understand—that you understand what's happened."

"All right," said Marshall, and he sat on the couch beside Priscilla.

Matt pulled a rocker around so that he could sit directly in front of them and look them in the eyes as he talked.

"I was trying to pray—just this morning, though it seems like days ago—trying to sort through the mess I'd made of things and one verse of Scripture kept running through my mind. It was, 'You have no part or share in this ministry because your heart is not right before God.'

"I looked it up in Acts 8. Simon the Sorcerer had offered the apostles money in exchange for spiritual power. At first I thought, *That's not me. I'd never offer God money for power; I'm not that ignorant.*

"But then the Lord seemed to say, 'No, not money, but something even more valuable—your family.' I remembered the evening at Chen's, when Profett first asked me to work for him. I was so excited that my Bradbury was paying off and I was at last going to get the position and recognition I deserved. From that moment on—I'm ashamed to admit it, but it's true—I sacrificed my family, and especially you, Priscilla, for the sake of position and power." As he spoke her name, Matt reached out and touched her arm but she drew away from him. Though it cut him like a knife, he understood it and made no more of it.

"This morning in prayer," Matt continued, "I still tried to convince myself that sacrificing you was what I had to do. Profett had shown me where Jesus said it was necessary that a man 'hate' even his wife and children for the Lord's sake. But then it hit me like a bolt of light. Jesus said a man had to 'hate' even wife and children *for his sake;* Jesus never said to hate them for the sake of position and power.

"That was my first real insight into how wrong I had been. And how wrong John Profett was, too, since he fostered and fed my delusion."

Priscilla dabbed at the corners of her eyes with a tissue. "I guess only the Lord could have shown you that," she said. "I don't think you'd have listened to anyone else."

Matt nodded. "And that's not all he showed me. I went back to the very beginning, to the Malachi prophecy that Profett claimed to fulfill.

'See, I will send you the prophet Elijah before that great and dreadful day of the Lord comes.'

"I read on. 'He will turn the hearts of the fathers to their children, and the hearts of the children to their fathers.'

"When those words sank in, I could hardly believe my eyes. I read them again and again, just letting their meaning penetrate. Then I wondered where in the world my head had been when I read the passage before. Somehow, in all those times, and in all the complicated discussions with learned theolo-gians, not once had I seen it.

"It was almost as if scales fell from my eyes, Marshall." Matt addressed this part directly to his father-in-law to include him in his explanation. "I saw that Profett had done *exactly the opposite* of what this Scripture said Elijah would do. He had turned the members of our family against each other instead of bringing us together."

Marshall nodded but said nothing.

Matt turned toward Priscilla again. "I knew then that John Profett was no Elijah and that Diane had been right when she told me the man had to be either crazy or evil.

"Once I knew that—well, scenes from these past few weeks played in my mind like videos, and I soon suspected exactly what Profett did. I took my evidence to Captain Drake, and the rest, as they say, is history."

Matt paused for a deep breath.

Marshall spread out his hands toward Priscilla and Matt. "Amazing, isn't it," he said, "what we can learn from the Bible when we read what it actually says?"

Matt nodded in silent agreement. "Priscilla," he said, and she lifted her eyes to his face. "Can you—will you forgive me?"

"Oh, Matt, I've felt so lonesome and abandoned without you these past few weeks. Of course I forgive you," she said.

Moments later they were in each other's arms as a smiling Marshall hugged them both.

"I know what Drake wants us to do," she told Matt a bit later. "He told Dad and me all about it when he called. Matt, I want to help."

"Are you sure?" Matt implored. "I don't know if I can stand to see you in the same room with that man." Matt looked at her, anguished. "Without wanting to kill him."

"The object," Priscilla reminded him, "is to take Profett out of circulation without destroying ourselves. I think you can manage your anger if it will accomplish that. And I can face seeing him again as long as I know where you stand. Please, Matt, let me help; it's the only way."

"Okay, then," said Matt, "we'll do it, because I don't ever intend to let you doubt where I stand again."

31

At precisely two the next afternoon, Larry's Olds 442 pulled up in front of the Douglas residence. Larry scrambled out from behind the steering wheel, hurrying around to open the passenger door for Profett. But Profett had already emerged and was standing on the curb.

Matt watched from his living room window with consternation as the two of them started for his front door. "That's Larry Forrester, my daughter's boyfriend, with Profett," he told the concealed Captain Drake in a stage whisper. "What's he doing here? He's going to foul up everything!"

"No, he's not," hissed Drake. "We can handle it. Just stick to the plan."

"Hello, Matt," said John Profett, smiling, when Matt answered his ring at the front door moments later. "I didn't think you'd mind if I brought Larry along. He's joining us full time as my personal assistant. He'll be in on everything from now on."

"Hello, Larry," said Matt. "I must say, this is quite a surprise."

"Isn't it great?" said Larry. "The three of us, working together!"

Profett swept past Matt and greeted Priscilla in the living room. "I'm so glad to see you back home and feeling better," he said as he took her by the hand.

Priscilla wilted as Profett plied her with his oily phrases. For a moment Matt feared she would crack. He was momentarily sorry that she had come, but she quickly recovered.

As everyone took a comfortable seat in the living room, Profett continued. "Well, Matt, what was it you and Priscilla wanted to discuss? If there's any way I can accommodate your needs, I'll certainly do it. You two mean a lot to me."

The smoothness of the man infuriated Matt. Once more the purple rage grew behind his eyes and he thought of the gun still cached away in David's drawer. For a moment he wished he was carrying it so he could live out the scenario he had only imagined before—all nine shots emptied into Profett's head and chest. *Thank God I'm not alone here with him or I'd probably do it,* Matt thought. *In fact, I wouldn't need a gun; I could strangle him with my bare hands.*

Be cool, Matt ordered himself. *You have to keep control if you expect to have any chance to nail this guy.*

"I'm afraid things have gone too far," said Matt calmly. "I'm no longer able to serve John Profett Ministries." He looked Profett straight in the eye. "The fact is, I no longer want to. I see things a lot differently than I did even a day or two ago."

"Matt, Matt, you can't mean that," said Profett. "After all we've been through together? We're a winning team, Matt. You wouldn't let Satan break up our team!"

Matt put his arm around Priscilla who was sitting beside him on the couch. "Priscilla and I are the team I'm concerned about," he said.

"May I remind you," Profett said coldly, "that you wouldn't even have Priscilla if I hadn't saved her life? You know, the Bible says, 'If a man pays back evil for good, evil will never leave his house.' You owe me, Matt. Both of you owe me. And if you treat me like this, you're consigning your house to a curse that will never leave. Do you understand me? Never!"

"Well, we just don't happen to see it that way," said Matt.

Profett hung his head and stared at the floor. When he looked back up he had tears in his eyes. "Forgive me," he said as he wiped the corner of one eye with his forefinger. "I just can't believe this is happening. I trusted you, Matt. I thought you were my friend. I've told

you things about me that I've never shared with another human being."
He shook his head slowly like a man in great sorrow. "I just don't
understand it."

Larry was buying Profett's act one hundred percent, and he stared
at Matt with an incredulous how-could-you expression. For a fleeting
moment, even Matt couldn't help feeling pity for Profett, in spite of
all he knew. What a colossal actor the man was! *When this tactic
doesn't work, I wonder what he'll try next,* Matt thought.

He didn't wait long to find out.

"Did I misjudge you, Matt?" Profett was saying now. "I thought
you were a man of vision, a man with a heart for God's work. Didn't
you tell me not long ago that the Elijah Project had given meaning to
your existence like you never knew before in your entire life? I made
you part of the biggest event in history, Matt. Most Christians would
die for the opportunity I've given you. Larry here has told me he would
even pass up the NFL to work with me, and do it gladly."

Larry was nodding in vigorous agreement, and Matt could see the
unspoken appeal in his eyes for Matt to come to his senses. *Poor Larry,*
thought Matt, sickened. *Another puppet on a string for Profett.*

"Can I say something?" Priscilla had endured Profett's theatrics in
silence, but now she spoke. "Larry, you know our family. You know
what we were before John Profett came along, and you know what has
become of us since. Jesus said to beware of false prophets and that
you can know them by their fruits. What has been the fruit in our
family, Larry? What?" Her eyes welled with tears. "Please, Larry,"
she pleaded, "don't go anywhere with this man. If you care anything
about us, if you care anything about Diane—"

Larry looked at her icily as he interrupted. "I'm not about to get led
astray by the spirit of Jezebel," he said.

"That's enough!" Matt's eyes were blazing and he jumped to his
feet. "Nobody will sit in my house and call my wife or my daughter a
Jezebel ever again." He turned from Larry to Profett. "Do you understand me?" he demanded. "Nobody!"

Profett leaped to his feet also. "Jezebel's weasel husband Ahab had more guts than you'll ever have," he shouted. "When I get through with you, you won't have a house to sit in or anything else."

"That may be," said Matt, "knowing you. But I've made my decision. I'm calling a press conference right away to tell the world I've dissolved my association with John Profett, and I'll be telling them exactly why.

"Then I have some family ties to rebuild with two beautiful women who never had your so-called spirit of Jezebel, but do have the spirit of Christ."

Matt turned to Larry, who was also now standing. "Profett is right about one thing; Christ is coming again and it may be soon. But don't make the mistake I did and lose sight of something else quite wonderful. Christ is already here. He's been living in our hearts and our home for a long time. Thank God he hasn't moved out, even during the recent madness, but he is soon going to feel a lot more at home again."

"That is a lovely speech," said Profett, "but I really can't allow you to damage the work of God with your treachery."

"And just how do you plan to stop me?"

"Not me," said Profett. "God. You should remember what happens to people who oppose God and me. At Mount Carmel, God sent down fire from heaven to back me up, and 450 prophets of Baal ended up dead."

At this implied threat, Captain Drake and his officers poised themselves to intervene. Instead of attempting violence, however, Profett beckoned Larry and walked to the door. "Goodbye, prophet of Baal," he told Matt, "and I do mean goodbye!" Then he was gone.

Matt stood there trembling, not from fear but from anger. Profett had escaped their trap. He had been within their grasp, and had walked away scot-free. Not only that, but he had taken Larry—his newest victim—with him.

Matt turned to take Priscilla in his arms as Captain Drake and his two officers emerged from their hiding places.

"I'm sorry," Matt told Drake. "He's just too slippery."

Drake nodded. "Slippery guys slip up sooner or later," he said grimly. "I just wish it would be sooner."

"At least we can be happy he has done all the damage he's ever going to do around this house," said Matt, giving Priscilla, whom he still held in his arms, a squeeze.

"Well," said Drake. "There's nothing more we can do here. You have probably seen the last of Mr. Profett. But just in case he has something else in mind, Officer Crane will be observing the house for a while from an unmarked van across the street."

Matt and Crane nodded at each other, and the policemen left. As soon as they were gone, Matt went to the phone. "I'm calling the press right now," he told Priscilla. "I'm sure they—" He stopped in mid-sentence. "That's strange," he said. "I can't get a dial tone." He checked the connections to the wall jack and to his answering machine. Everything looked good.

"I don't like this one bit," said Matt. He stepped to the window and looked out. The van was still there. Maybe Crane could protect them and maybe he couldn't. Matt went to David's room, opened his desk drawer, drew out his Luger and loaded a full clip of nine bullets.

"Try the bedroom phone or your office," suggested Priscilla. "Maybe just this one telephone is out of order." She followed a few steps behind as he walked down the hall to his office. Matt picked up the receiver there and found it dead also. *When could he have cut my phone line?* Matt thought. *Could he have done it on his way out?*

Suddenly Profett's last words repeated in his mind. "I can't allow you to damage the work of God . . . remember what happens to people who oppose me . . . fire from heaven . . . ended up dead."

Matt had been about to hang up the dead telephone but now he froze with his hand in midair. If Profett had cut his phone line, what else might he have done? He couldn't possibly have had time to firebomb his house or car. Could he?

Matt shook his head. He couldn't have. At least not just now. But Profett had been in his home often in the past, sometimes all alone. Was it possible—? The man was nothing if not diabolically clever.

Suddenly Matt dropped the receiver, leaving it dangling at the end of its cord. He grabbed a surprised Priscilla and pushed her down the hall toward the front door. "Come on!" he yelled.

"Wait!" she protested as they reached the door. "It's raining! At least let me get a jacket." She pulled away to stop at the entry closet.

"There's no time for that!" Matt yelled. He grabbed her arm in an iron grip and propelled her out the door, straight across the flower bed and lawn of their front yard, and into the street.

They had barely reached the far curb when the house behind them exploded in an immense fireball. Officer Crane was out the van door and sprinting to their prostrate forms instantly. Up and down the street neighbors poured from houses with shattered windows to see what had caused the big blast.

By now, Matt and Priscilla were slowly getting to their feet. "Are you all right?" Crane asked as he looked them over carefully.

"We are all right," said Matt, "but could you take care of calling the fire department? I have another urgent call to make."

From a neighbor's phone, Matt called two major broadcasters and the *Oregonian*. "I'm Matt Douglas," he said, "until today the director of John Profett Ministries. My house just exploded and I hold John Profett responsible. Be here by four o'clock and you'll get quite a story."

He hung up the phone and took a pale, still-trembling Priscilla in his arms again. "I'm so sorry!" he said. "After all I've put you through, and now you don't even have your house anymore. And with Christmas almost here."

She clung to him. "But I have you," she said, "and together I feel like we can handle anything."

Priscilla turned to Jill Farmsly, her neighbor. "Now, can I use the phone?" she asked. "I need to let family know we're okay. If they hear about the explosion on the news, they will be frantic."

"Of course," said Jill, who had already covered Priscilla's cold, damp shoulders with a sweater, "and meanwhile I'll make you some nice hot tea."

Priscilla called her father first, then David, then Diane. At Diane's number, her roommate answered. "Diane isn't here," she told Priscilla. "Larry came by several hours ago insisting she go for a ride with him to try to work things out between them. She should have been back by now, but . . . shall I have her call you when she comes back?"

"Have her call her Grandfather Brown," said Priscilla, "just as soon as she can."

She hung up the phone and turned to Matt. "Diane's with Larry," Priscilla said, concern etched on her face. "He picked her up hours ago."

"Hours ago?" echoed Matt. "But Larry was just here with Profett. Where could Diane have been?"

Matt grabbed the phone and dialed the Sheridan Office Complex. Shelly answered just as if everything was normal.

"Shelly, this is Matt. You haven't seen my daughter Diane there, have you? She left school with her boyfriend this morning and we aren't sure where they went."

"She hasn't been here," said Shelly. "I did see Larry a while ago. He and Mr. Profett came in together just past noon. They said they were meeting with you at two. Didn't they show up?"

"They showed up all right," said Matt. "They really showed up, and my house exploded right after they left. Priscilla and I are lucky to be alive."

"What?" said Shelly. "You can't be serious."

"I've never been more serious in my life," said Matt, "but I can't take time to explain right now. I've got to find Diane. You say Profett and Larry came in together? You didn't see Profett all morning, then?"

"No," said Shelly, "he called about mid-morning and said he wouldn't be in for a while, that something had come up. Then, just as I was going out to lunch, I saw him arrive in the parking lot with Larry in Larry's car."

Matt thanked Shelly for the information and promised to tell her everything later. He then quickly said goodbye and dialed for Captain Drake. "You had Profett under surveillance," said Matt when he reached

Drake. "When and where did he get together with Larry Forrester before they came to our house?"

"Let's see," said Drake. "I'll check the report. Why do you ask?"

"I'm trying to trace his steps," said Matt, deciding he couldn't waste time telling Drake the whole story. Drake would only slow him down, or worse, sideline him entirely. "I guess you know my house blew up soon after you left."

"Yes," said Drake. "I heard. Okay, I guess you can know what we know about Profett's activities of the morning. He left his home in Colton at 10:13. He drove directly to Larry Forrester's residence in Garden Home, arriving there at 11:06. He entered and stayed until 11:34, when both he and Forrester emerged. They left in Forrester's car and went to your office at the Sheridan Complex, where they arrived at 12:09. Then—"

Matt had heard enough. He hung up, leaving Drake in mid-sentence with a dead telephone.

"She's at Larry's house," Matt told Priscilla. "I'm going out there."

"I'm going too," said Priscilla.

Matt hesitated. "It could be dangerous," he said. "Profett is probably there."

"If you're going, I'm going," said Priscilla.

"Kind of strong willed for a woman, aren't you?" Matt's tone and his small crooked smile said plainly that he meant the remark as a compliment. "Okay, let's go then!"

✳   ✳   ✳

Matt and Priscilla found both the green Olds and Profett's car at Larry's place. "Wait in the car," said Matt, "until I make sure everything's okay."

He walked up to the front door, pulled David's gun from his inside jacket pocket, quietly turned the knob and tested the door; it was not locked. Bursting in he trained his gun on a surprised Larry and on John Profett. Huddled in a corner of the couch sat Diane, her face streaked with tears.

"Dad!" she cried, "Thank God you've come!"

"Come over here away from those two," Matt instructed her as he kept the gun trained on the two men. Once she was at his side, he asked, "Are you okay? Did they hurt you?"

"My wrists are a little raw," she sobbed. "Larry held me and they tied me up!"

"Okay, go out to the car," said Matt. "Your mother is waiting there, and she'll be awfully glad to see you."

Diane wiped some of the tears away. "Aren't you coming, Dad?"

"I'll be along. Just give me a minute."

Matt couldn't decide what to do next. He wanted to just turn and leave and never see Profett or Larry again. But he knew Larry was an innocent in all of this. Somehow he had to try one more time to open the young man's eyes.

"Larry, why did you do this to Diane?" he finally asked.

Larry looked at Profett, then back at Matt. "It's for her own good," he said. "You and Mrs. Douglas have made your choice, but Diane is still young enough to be saved from the spirit of Jezebel if—"

"Larry," Matt interrupted, "did you know our house blew up right after you two left this afternoon?"

Larry just stood there slowly shaking his head.

"So, what do you think of your boss now?" Matt persisted. "Or do you approve of arson and murder in the name of Jesus?"

"Of course not," said Larry, "which is why I think you'd better put down that gun, Mr. Douglas." He moved toward Matt.

"Hold it right there," ordered Matt. "Don't come any closer."

"You'll have to shoot me," said Larry, still coming, "before you can shoot Mr. Profett."

Larry doesn't believe me, he thought. *But there's no way I can shoot him!*

Behind Larry, Profett drew a chrome revolver from under his clothes.

The next split second unfolded in slow motion. Larry's big fist crashed into Matt's jaw, and Matt's gun flew out the open front door. Matt collapsed to the floor as a tremendous explosion shook the small room. Larry's face contorted in agony as the bullet Profett had meant for Matt tore into Larry's back. He hit the ground hard, gurgling.

Then Profett was standing over Matt where he sprawled on the floor. "Fool!" spat Profett as he aimed the gun at Matt's head. "You have ruined everything."

A series of shots rang out. Matt cringed, hearing nine shots but not feeling the bullets. Profett looked surprised, then puzzled, then pained, then dazed, as he dropped the gun and slowly crumpled to the floor beside Matt.

Matt rolled over to see a shaking Priscilla still holding the gun. Behind her he saw Diane, hugging her mother before moving closer to help Larry.

Matt could see two or three bloody holes in Profett's chest. He made no sound, but Matt could see the blood welling and ebbing irregularly.

A siren howled nearby.

Epilogue

Marcel Tyrone Thorpe, alias John Profett, survived his wounds. He was tried and convicted of the murder of Richard E. Thomas and was sentenced to life imprisonment in the Oregon State Penitentiary.

Matt and Priscilla Douglas testified for the state in the prosecution and conviction of Marcel Tyrone Thorpe. They also organized and became full partners in Matt Douglas Investigations, an agency specializing in religious, political and consumer fraud.

Marshall Brown retired from his investment business and became senior advisor and principal owner of Matt Douglas Investigations.

Larry Forrester survived his wounds, realized how deceived he had been, and resumed his courtship of an at-first reluctant but ultimately forgiving Diane Douglas.

David Douglas entered college to train for a career in law enforcement.

Matt's angel stayed out of sight, but Matt knew he was still there.